VIEW FINDER

A NOVEL

Brandon,

VIEW FINDER

A NOVEL

Greg Jolley (signature)

GREG JOLLEY

Hope you enjoy BB's adventure. (handwritten inscription)

bhc
press

Livonia, Michigan

Editor: Amanda Lewis

Word definitions are taken from (1923) Webster's Unabridged Dictionary. Public domain.

VIEW FINDER
Copyright © 2019 Greg Jolley

Published by BHC Press

Library of Congress Control Number: 2018953897

ISBN: 978-1-64397-004-2 (Hardcover)
ISBN: 978-1-948540-17-9 (Softcover)
ISBN: 978-1-64397-005-9 (Ebook)

For information, write:
BHC Press
885 Penniman #5505
Plymouth, MI 48170

Visit the publisher:
www.bhcpress.com

ALSO BY GREG JOLLEY

Danser

Dot to Dot

The Amazing Kazu

Where's Karen?

Murder in a Very Small Town

Malice in a Very Small Town

Dedicated to

Jim Orosco,
Chief Construction Mechanic, USN, (ret).
(Seabee)

ACT ONE
REDWOOD

Savior
One who saves, preserves, or delivers from destruction or danger

Scene 1

Mumm and I and her film crew were in a caravan of cars driving north out of Hollywood. The two-lane road weaved along the coastline while she and I used sunlight to illuminate the interior view of our raised View-Masters. This was 1951 when automobiles were shaped like turtles with an additional hump.

Mumm's driver, Mr. Brenton, "Call me Brent," asked, "Enjoying the view?"

Neither of us replied. Mumm tapped my hand and I accepted the offered reel, *Grand Canyon*. I looked into the rearview mirror and saw Mr. Brenton was looking at Mumm the way most men did when they were so close to a breathing movie star. His eyes were furtive like a squinting woodchuck, and he had a greasy smile. If a gaze could breathe, his was sucking in Mumm. He tapped the ash tip off his cigarette out his vent window. I removed *Wild Animals of Africa*, inserted *Grand Canyon*, and aimed my View-Master to the sun and ocean to take in the view.

I laid *Africa* on the top of our lunch basket on the seat between us. The warm air entering the car smelled like sea salt. The scent was safe. Mr. Brenton spoke a few more times, I think, but whatever he said was like the noise of a ball game on the radio. Mumm and I viewed and shared slides in silence, and our caravan traveled further up into the California summer day.

Two hours later, our row of automobiles stopped for fuel at a service station. Mumm opened the basket while our driver and the film crew went inside to eat. She handed me a sandwich wrapped in wax paper and a bottle of cola, and we ate quietly with our View-Masters in our laps. For dessert, she unwrapped cellophane and offered me a blossom of orange wedges. I chose one, knowing better. I took a single breath from it and lost the next few minutes to spiraling confusion.

Since I was a boy, certain smells could send me off. I had taken the "nasty fall on my noggin," as Father explained it, when I was four. I had been to Mumm's doctor and specialists over the years, who I overheard talking to her about my "faulty synapses."

Mumm liked the studio team but wouldn't dine with them. She didn't want to be recognized in public. We were on what she called an *idyllic*—a rare adventure together.

After lunch, we placed the papers and bottles inside the basket, and Mumm asked to see the storyboards. I pulled my satchel up onto the seat and eased the white cardboard panels out. The story that we were traveling to film was told in my brief notes, sketched camera angles, and character silhouettes. Mumm asked for the first two panels and rested them in order from top to bottom on her lap. She traced her small finger from shot to shot of my latest rescue story, tracing the inked dialogue in my drawings and reading them aloud in her soft British accent.

"Your story defines a new twist on *saving*." She smiled.

I was pleased. She asked for the next two panels and read them silently with her fingertip save for one question about transition. She asked her questions softly, and her thoughts were focused and concerned. And kind. She and I went through all the storyboards to the last, which she knew I wouldn't share. She handed me the panels, and I slid them back inside the satchel. Mumm pointed to the open carryall, to the letters bound with a green ribbon.

"How is *that* mystery going, darling?" she asked.

"I received a new letter last Wednesday."

There were bothersome dust motes in the warm air of the rear seat. I looked away from Mumm to the tan fabric of the car door beside me.

"Do you know where she is yet?" she asked gently.

I rolled my window down and breathed in the fresh air.

"I think so, yes. She's near a town called Greenland. I found the town on my map, but I don't know where the house is."

"Is she still in danger? Are you planning to go to her? To save her?"

I frowned at the door fabric.

"I want to, yes. But I think I'm too young."

I turned to Mumm and watched her consider. She and I had talked of the letters before, about the mystery and concerns for the girl, but this was the first time we had spoken of a possible next step, an actual rescue attempt. I looked at Mumm's beautiful gray-blue eyes and watched how her pensive expression tilted the right side of her lips into a rare smile that, when shared, had stolen millions of hearts.

She was poised to speak, and I was eager to hear her hopefully encourage me on, but the film crew was spilling out of the diner, animated and laughing, making their way to their cars and ours. Mumm raised a finger to her lips and breathed over it. "Darling BB, later."

I nodded, feeling sad, but I understood. Our car jostled, and Mr. Brenton climbed in behind the wheel. Mumm leaned forward and spoke to him while I closed my satchel. When I looked up, Mr. Brenton was handing Mumm a scarf, sunglasses, and a wide-brow fedora. I watched her put them on while Mr. Brenton climbed back out and circled to Mumm's door to open it. He followed Mumm to the diner and then to the side yard to the restroom door, which he opened. After inspecting the interior, he stepped back for her to enter.

He took up a position in front of the door, scanning the side yard and road. I heard our other automobiles starting up and took my View-Master from the seat and began to sort through the slides. Inside the next three-dimensional reel, a lion was bounding through tall grass toward a deer that was peacefully unaware.

• • • •

OUR SUNLIGHT melted into the sea. A while later, the road climbed into the foothills, and I turned on the dome light. Mumm and I View-Mastered using that light as our train of cars rose higher and higher. When I looked out my window between reel changes, the evening was a medium blue, and tall oaks and pines had replaced the foothill grasses. The safe scent of pine trees colored the cool air coming in through my window in good contrast to the heat from earlier.

Before I raised my View-Master, I turned to Mumm, who was relaxing sideways against her door with her beautiful face raised, her slight pale hands elevated, holding her viewer toward the amber dome light. She was viewing *Scenic Mexico*.

"BB, tell me about the new letter?" she asked, not lowering her viewer.

I set my viewer down and took up my satchel. Mumm knew the backstory, how I had seen *her* first post in the letters column in the third issue of the comic *Black Kisses*.

Right off, I was enticed by seeing a letter from a girl in a comic—most of the letters I read, and I read all that I could, were from guys.

"She is beautiful and ripe with lust. So am I," was how the girl described the femme fatale.

Lust really caught my eye. *Ripe* made my emotions swirl. After her first paragraph, she went off the tracks.

"Foggy from medications, frightening dreams, the ropes have burned my skin."

She closed with a plea for help and signed, "Luscious."

In response, the *Black Kisses'* editor wrote, "Looks like we have one reader who needs help getting untangled and *plucked* from danger." Plucked. I recall spending hours refining my ideas about that verb.

I wrote to *Black Kisses,* and they actually published my letter citing it as one of a million other offers to rescue the *damsel*. It is clear to me now that the magazine was treating her plight tongue-in-cheek, pleased by the attention and increased sales.

When her second letter was posted, it made no pretense to address the story or the art of the new issue of *Black Kiss*. She repeated her plea for help in fearful and seductive language promising a "sensual and warm reward."

I was hooked. So were many others. The letters column normally carried four topics to spark readers' interest, but this issue only read, "Will You Help Our Seductive Damsel?"

I penned a second letter, this one to the editor asking that it not be published. Instead, I asked for the girl's address. I wrote out my worries for her safety and included my willingness to save her. I didn't mention the reward she offered, but it was close to my heart. They published my letter anyway along with five others from guys who had similar hopes and designs.

The editor had the last word. When the next issue came out, he explained to the readers that the girl had, in fact, been rescued and went on to suggest five new topics of discussion.

I knew better by then. I had received a letter from her. It included her address.

I wrote to her in a passion. I offered to save her or die trying. I didn't mention the reward, but she brought it up when she penned her reply.

"I'm losing sleep and days because of the medications. I'm so frightened. Almost all my clothing is missing. Please hurry. Untie me, save me. My swelling breasts and luscious lips await you."

The correspondence continued. I had shared this with Mumm. Well, most of it.

Now in the car on the winding road with Mumm beside me, I removed the most recent envelope and opened the letter, which was lavender perfumed like the others. The pale purple scent was troublesome, causing me to spiral when breathed from too deeply.

"She wrote out directions," I said. "And drew a map."

Mumm asked for the letter, and I handed it to her knowing that, like with the others, she wouldn't read it. Mumm breathed from the paper and responded with a secretive smile. "You're not too young, my love. You're fourteen. And a rescue would be admirable."

I felt relief. No, I felt lifted. My half-planned thoughts about how to get to Greenland, California, began to swim and consolidate.

"I will have to smooth this for your father."

I deflated downward, down into the reality of being fourteen and having a father with a quick temper and quicker fists.

Father had what would later be described as an anger issue. IM, as he insisted everyone call him, didn't approve of Mumm's or my absence from what he referred to as "our cocoon." I traveled directly between school and home, and Mumm was escorted at a quick drive between the studio and the mansion and the evening dinners and events.

The current *idyllic* Mumm and I were on was a rare break from the cocoon and made possible by IM being away for four days—he had accepted an emergency lighting job on a shoot in Yelapa, Mexico. It seems that the lighting of a few key exterior shots required his expertise. A half-hour after he left for the airport, Mumm had green flagged, as they say during movie preproduction, our trip. She and Mr. Nash had chosen the crew and off we went.

We rode in silence for a few miles. I looked out my window into the real world. I saw a road sign that read "Santa Cruz—9 Miles."

Mumm held her viewer in one hand and rested her other on my knee. I breathed from the letter one last time, slid it within the green ribbon holding the others, and stowed them in my satchel.

The road grew steeper and the turns tighter. When our car stopped, Mr. Brenton said, "I'll go check," and I listened to him open and close his door. I looked up and watched him appear in our headlights, walking to the lead car, where he spoke to the driver.

The front car was turned off the road and into the entrance of a driveway that rose steeply into the trees. Flickering lanterns defined the driveway's edges as it rose to a hilltop residence. A man dressed in white appeared behind the gate, unlocked it, and walked it open. Mr. Brenton climbed back in behind the wheel, and our train of four cars rolled up to the house.

We came to a stop in the center of a curve under a trellised awning of redwood beams. On Mumm's side of the car, wide steps rose to an expansive landing and open double doors that offered a warm, welcoming light. Another man in white stood up there and waved as Mr. Brenton circled and opened Mumm's door. She handed me her viewer and eased off her seat. Mr. Brenton followed her up the stairs, three steps back as usual, and they went inside.

I collected all our slides and our viewers and stowed them in my satchel. The film crew was climbing out and mixing at the base of the stairs with their suitcases. The other three automobiles were moved to the parking area a short way past the house. Mumm's automobile remained at the base of the stairs for her use, if necessary.

After Mumm had been escorted inside, the film crew and I reverted to a first-name basis. For them, Mr. Mayer became *Ezra,* and I was no longer addressed as Mr. Danser but instead as my first name, BB. There were seven of us, and the mood was light and fun as we climbed the wide stairs as a group and entered the massive foyer.

A different man dressed in white welcomed us and asked that we leave our suitcases there in the entrance. He then asked if we were prepared to dine or preferred to freshen up first. The consensus was, "Let's eat."

Mumm was nowhere to be seen, but I was used to this happening—certain that our hosts had whisked her away for their exclusive enjoyment.

I went out to Mumm's car and retrieved my wicker Samsonite from the truck. When I was back inside, I saw the tail end of the crew entering tall glass doors that I assumed, correctly, was a dining room.

The dinner table was long enough for twenty, and the crew had taken to the far end, where most sat with their backs to the wall of full bookcases. The room was elegant—the table was lit by candles under glass, the dinnerware was a simple gold China, and a light piano sonata fell from speakers set in the ceiling.

I took the chair at the edge of the crew. Ezra said grace, and dinner was served by four young waiters in white. The meal was excellent, and the conversation was quick and random, weaving through many topics at once. There was a lot of joking and warmth. Only Ezra was focused, asking the others technical questions about the next day's shoot. I took the storyboards from my satchel, and they circled among the crew in sequential order as we ate.

I knew I was being treated with kid gloves and indulged as the son of the famous actress, Elizabeth Stark—only I called her Mumm, at her insistence. At the production meeting and meal before we left Hollywood, the crew's questions went to her until she asked, one time only, that they be addressed to me. The film crew was treating this one-day shoot seriously, and each of them applied their expertise to the discussion.

After dessert and coffee, our lead technician excused himself. He would be working most of the night running power and water to the set as well as unloading our equipment trailer.

A waiter came in with a plate of room keys and handed them out. He apologized for the residence, which was one room short of accommodating all of us separately. Ezra offered to share his, and I raised my hand. We all headed upstairs. I paused halfway up, looking deeper into the house, wondering where Mumm and our hosts were. I knew, having watched the canisters carefully loaded, that a current Elizabeth Stark film had been packed to be shown. The house was quiet, and I saw a waiter seated beside a tall fern and double doors and decided he was at the ready if our hosts or Mumm needed anything.

There was a fireplace in our room, and I liked that and insisted, as best a teenager could, that Ezra take the bed and allow me to have the couch before the fire.

• • • •

LATE IN the night, I was woken by the sound of distant laughter and confusion and perhaps dinnerware and furniture being moved about. I didn't hear Mumm's voice, which would have contrasted with the Americanized English.

When I woke again at dawn, Ezra was already gone. I dressed to the sounds of the crew's conversations out in the hall. I headed downstairs with the others but turned away from them as they made their way to the dining room.

I opened the double doors to what I believed was the screening room and confirmed my assumption. It was an ascending room with couches aligned downward, enough seating to accommodate sixteen. The room was lit by dim lights that glowed downward on the golden walls.

At the base of the room, three men were clearing the dining table centered on the stage before the movie screen. As if on cue, the projector came on and cast a rectangle of white light on the men and the clutter of toppled chairs and the table littered with the previous night's serving trays, dinners, glassware, and bottles, some tipped over and a few on the ground. The once-white tablecloth was stained and madly uneven, pulled hard to one end as though someone had attempted that old magic trick. And failed.

The men in the light from the projector looked ghostly. I opened my satchel and found my hand-me-down Tewe director's lens. Raising it to my eye, I composed the image of their efforts framing the stage.

A silver cart appeared in the composition from the right side of the stage pushed by a waiter. It was a vignette of white and silver and conflicting shadows on the big screen. The men worked slowly as though familiar with cleaning up after a prior night's chaos.

"Just like at home." I recalled the nightly antics of Father and his friends and studio peers at Mumm's mansion in Inglewood. I viewfound until the projector went dark, and its faint clicking and humming ended. I pressed the Tewe back inside my satchel and left the room.

In the dining room, Ezra and Mr. Nash and our 3D cameraman sat before their breakfasts drawing in pencil on the storyboards and discussing the pencil strokes. The rest of the film crew had already headed out, leaving behind cleaned breakfast plates and emptied glasses.

I sat down beside Ezra and was served breakfast which I quickly ate while listening to two of the men talk of angles, frames, and pans. Their conversation changed to decisions on how best to use the minimal props to satisfy the dual 3D cameras that Mr. Nash would be operating. After a couple of minutes, Mr. Nash asked me to stop bobbing my head to their cadence.

I stopped tracing the lines of their discussion. I wanted to stay and listen and learn. I also knew that it was better to be with the crew on set doing what I could to be helpful. The technician who had worked all night entered the room. I left with him, leaving the table quietly, not asking to be excused because I didn't want to interrupt Ezra and Mr. Nash.

The film set was easy to find—I followed the electrical and water lines from the house into the towering redwoods on the opposite end of the driveway. The cables and hoses led down along brick steps through the fragrant shadows. The redwoods rose like legs up to skirts of green.

With ferns brushing my pant legs, I safely breathed the musk of the dark red bark.

I walked on and found the set, the *mise en scène*, as Mr. Nash preferred, located just past the equipment cases a few yards before a clearing. The 3D cameras were set up, and the lighting panels were arranged. Two boomed microphones were extended—one back into the trees and the second aimed out into the clearing. The script called for capturing the different kinds of wind we hoped would rise from the sea. Mr. Lillison, known to the crew as Lilly, was at the soundboard tapping dials and making notes on a clipboard.

A trolley track had been laid out for the dual cameras. In the studio, a crane would be used, but this would work fine, and it had to—we had little time.

Where they would usually wear just one hat, each member of the small crew covered multiple roles while other tasks not vital to the production had been discarded. Mumm and Ezra had selected the members of the team carefully during the production meeting for my short four-minute film.

Mr. Nash and Ezra stepped from the shadows and ferns and entered the set. Everyone got busier—silent and focused—and settled two steps back from our director, Mr. Nash. I aligned my eyes with the cameras.

Mumm sat on a kitchen chair in the buttery meadow. She appeared half submerged in the golden grass, her chin tilted down, and her face obscured by fallen hair. Her once-golden hair was dyed black to match the gown she'd chosen for the film. Her aide, Mr. Siad, was shading her with an umbrella. He had a basket in his other hand, and I knew from experience what was in it—Mumm always had the same snacks available when filming—chilled bottles of Perrier and an imported tin of biscuits. Mr. Siad was smiling and trying to chat up Mumm who was keeping her head down.

Beyond the meadow was a cliff and the ocean. The first breeze of the day stirred the tall grass after humming through the redwoods.

Mr. Siad carried Mumm's umbrella and basket off the set and into the darkness of the trees. Mr. Nash looked the crew over, and when he looked through me, I saw that he was smirking, bright-eyed, and pleased to be in a director's chair for the first time. He spoke crisply to Mr. Carl, our gaffer and grip, and Mr. Carl stepped before the cameras and clacked the slate. Because we only had one day to film the entire four minutes, the schedule called for a sequential shoot.

We began.

Shot One: A scenic pan. From the deep blue ocean to the yellow silk meadow. Composition: The end of the meadow draws a horizontal line two-thirds up in the frame.

Shot Two: Mumm's chest and falling hair above the swaying grass. Medium-distance shot: The grass, her form, and the ocean.

Shot Three: Mumm's lovely and pale arms contrasted against her black dress. Close-up: A three-quarter angle.

Shot Four: A close-up of her delicate, soft white wrists.

Shot Five: The grass sways across the bottom third of the shot. Mumm hears something and doesn't raise her head but turns to the camera—a pull back.

Shot Six: Mumm's beautiful face in a close-up. Her eyes are tightened down, and yet still lovely. She unfolds and releases a beautiful smile, a smile of relief.

Shot Seven: I'm cued and do my slow walk on, my back to the camera as I enter the grass and the sunlight. I walk toward Mumm's grateful smile. Medium shot: My back enters and progresses from the right.

Shot Eight: Mumm's eyes turn to my side, my hip. Her expression changes. It is complex, a mixture of acceptance, and, possibly, understanding. Facial close-up.

Shot Nine: My back, my slow stride closer to Mumm, who is to my left. She continues to study my approach. Medium shot: Like shot seven.

Shot Ten: A close-up of my hip and arm and clothing as I walk closer.

Shot Eleven: Panning, lowering to my hand brushing through the grass holding a coil of rope.

Mr. Nash called for a fifteen-minute lunch break. Mr. Siad entered the set with Mumm's umbrella and basket as he had done between the prior eleven shots and reshoots over the past five hours.

Waiters dressed in white stepped from the redwoods with box lunches and distributed them among our crew. We ate quietly, the wind in the treetops and across the meadow more pronounced than our voices.

The film crew returned to their places with two minutes left on the break. I watched Mr. Ira Gersham adjusting the lighting panels between Mumm and the redwoods, and I took my mark as Mr. Siad retreated. Mr. Nash called, "Places and quiet," and Mr. Carl clacked the clapboard before the two cameras.

"Roll it."

A loud and angry voice came down through the trees. It was a voice I knew well—proud, demanding, and barking commands. Because no cut had been called, I stayed in role as did Mumm until the light from the canvas panels shifted and went dull.

"Cut!" Mr. Nash called. "IM? What the fuck do you think you're doing? *No*, what are you doing *here*?"

I turned to the tree line where Father had shoved Mr. Gersham and his panels to the ground causing arcs of light to sweep the set and crew. Father took hold of one of the panels, raised it, and changed its angle and the light it reflected. He studied the effect on Mumm's profile and grimaced and threw the panel back into the tall grass.

"No one lights *her* but me!" he yelled.

Although a cut had been called, Ezra kept the cameras rolling. Mr. Nash was up and out of his canvas chair and striding to Father, his voice equally hot and loud, and I watched Mr. Siad enter the meadow toward Mumm. I discretely let the coil of rope fall from my hand.

Mr. Siad kneeled before Mumm and untied her in the shade of the umbrella. When Mumm stood, he handed her an opened bottle of her sparkling water. She and Mr. Siad crossed the field of yellow grass and entered the redwoods, neither of them speaking or looking to the loud argument between Father and Mr. Nash. I watched her until the shadows and ferns hid her from view. Her departure was a tactic. It said that we were done with the filming even though the final scene had yet to be shot.

• • • •

I HELPED the crew break down the set and equipment after Father stomped off into the redwoods with Mr. Nash at his heels, both of them hollering. It took us four trips to get everything up to the house on top of the hill.

Mumm's automobile was gone, and I was sure she was behind the wheel beside Mr. Siad. She liked to drive, especially when disturbed. She rarely got a chance because of the contractual rules of the studio and Father's fear for her safety, or his fear of her being injured and unable to work.

We loaded the equipment into the trailer and the cars. Father's limousine was idling in the shade of the atrium where Mumm's car had been. Father was in the back seat, his door open, his voice loud, ranting.

"Those two fucking nutcakes! Running off to play while I slave!"

He was berating the driver who sat stone-faced and nodding in deference.

I expected to be ordered into Father's car, but his driver spun the tires on our host's driveway. I asked Ezra if I could ride with him and Mr. Nash.

The other three cars departed when we climbed into Mr. Nash's. Ezra took the wheel, and Mr. Nash and I shared the back seat. A waiter had set a basket inside, and it rested on the seat between us.

Ezra drove carefully and slowly down through the Santa Cruz Mountains. When we reached the highway, Mr. Nash opened the basket, and I opened my satchel. I felt around inside for my Tewe director's lens, planning on viewfinding the passing view from the perspective of the enclosed interior. There were redwoods to the left, and the ocean was a 180-degree pan to my right.

Mr. Nash ate, not offering anything to Ezra or myself, and I viewfound until our first stop for fuel. While Ezra pumped gasoline, Mr. Nash said, "Something's gonna be done about that father of yours."

I lowered my director's lens and blinked my eyes tight and fast, ending the film I was making.

"That's right. I'll talk and plan. You just bob your head as usual. Damn fool is great with light and lighting, but he has visions of grandeur, visions of—no, delusions—of control and importance."

I nodded and stowed my director's lens inside my satchel.

"If he wasn't on your mother's teat. Excuse that, he'd be out on his ear."

I looked up and was pleased that Ezra had done a fine job spraying the windshield with blue liquid from a bottle. Clean glass for clear viewing was important to me.

"What IM doesn't know, but I'll tell you so that you can prepare, is that he's being assigned full-time to the Yelapa shoot. The entire six weeks. So, you and I need to work together. For your mother."

I watched Ezra thoroughly wipe the windshield with blue paper towels.

"While he's away, I've arranged to have all of his belongings removed from her home."

He paused, and Ezra stepped back to admire his efforts.

"IM will be served divorce papers in Yelapa. She's finally come around and sees that he's a disaster, poison to her. Affecting her career and...you."

Ezra climbed in behind the wheel, and Mr. Nash said to me, "Let's talk about something else."

Ezra steered us back out onto the highway.

"Ezra? Do you think we could schedule and shoot the final scene in the studio?" Before Ezra could respond, Mr. Nash directed, "Chew on it for a few miles."

We drove along the highway in silence for three miles. When Ezra answered, he was looking at Mr. Nash in the rearview mirror.

"I would need to study the full storyboard. BB, can you describe your last secret scene?"

I did.

Mr. Nash turned to me with one brow arched. He breathed out heavily and reacted.

"Moses in a short skirt."

He and Ezra began talking the shot over—how it could be done in the studio since it only involved my hands and Mumm in close-up.

Ezra eyed me in the mirror. "If I may, it explains—defines—the title, *Savior*. I admire the dual meaning now that I can *see* the final shot."

"Savior has *two* meanings?" Mr. Nash asked.

"Yes. A savior is often the one who saves. But also consider the efforts of a *collector*."

Scene 2

Sixteen days later, I was down in the basement of Mumm's mansion in my *laboratory* as she affectionately called it. I was set up in one of three storerooms below ground. The walls were exposed beams, and my four rough wooden tables created an L-shape. There were standing lamps and the couch where I often slept. I had rolled out rugs on the concrete pad for warmth and borrowed seven standing mirrors from the furniture storeroom.

My camera, films, View-Masters, and reels were in neat order on the tables. A ground-level, high window faced west, and I often used its light in the evening for my View-Mastering. I had a desk containing my store-bought reels and the ones I produced with my 3D camera and reel construction kit. On the east wall of the lab, there was a ten-by-fourteen-foot movie screen of white canvas. My 3D projectors were side by side on a cart against the table.

The door to the room was locked, as always. I was sitting at the table with my stationary set, letters, magazines, comic collection, and my map and notes. The map was open to Northern California. The area at the base of the Sierras had an inked circle around it.

My satchel was open, and my bow-tied letters from Luscious were on top.

Because of the locked door, there was a row of five covered meal trays on the left side of the doorframe. My seven mirrors stood strategically to the sides of the entrance.

I wrote with the faint sounds of the humming air conditioning unit I shared with the basement. Music, laughter, and voices were coming through the vents above my head. The rhythm and melody of the sounds were interrupted by the heavy chain and motor of the service elevator descending.

When I heard the elevator door slide open, I closed the cover of my writing pad and capped my pen. I listened to the footfalls, recognized them, and unlocked the door.

Ezra entered with a box in his hand. It was the size of a shoebox and wrapped in an elegant matte of complex patterns. He was dressed formally and, as usual, looked uncomfortable in the attire required for the party upstairs. I watched his expression in the angled mirrors. In the frames, I could see 360-degrees of him, and more, if I considered the mirror echoes.

"Happy Birthday, BB. Fifteen is a big deal."

I thanked him, and he handed me the richly wrapped gift.

"Mind if I sit?" he asked.

I nodded and smiled.

Ezra studied the room before taking a seat on the couch. I set the gift on the table, sat in my chair, and swiveled it around.

"The party—your party—is at a simmer. Closing in on boiling." His smile looked weary.

That year, the parties were a nightly event. Father and his male friends and their *dates* drank and dined and drank and argued late into the night and beyond. Sometimes furniture was broken. Sometimes there were screams followed by wild laughter.

"Are you going to dress?" Ezra asked, looking at my formal clothing set out beside him on the couch.

"No," I said and walked to the seven mirrors. I looked at all 360-degrees of myself. I wore green serge pants, a gray shirt buttoned to the top, and my black gabardine vest—fully buttoned. My lean face was pale under my straight, black hair. My eyebrows were black and my nose straight. I didn't look into my eyes.

"I agree. You look fine," he said.

I raised my eyes and looked at him in the mirrors.

"And every day more like Peck." He believed I resembled the actor, Gregory Peck.

I returned to the chair, and Ezra stood and crossed to the projector carts where my dual 3D projectors were set beside the standard film player. He took up the top two film cans from the stack and read from their sides.

"New?" he asked.

"3D *and* a detective mystery," I agreed.

"This isn't in the theatres yet."

"Right. Mumm had them delivered for me. They're unedited. Would you like to view?" I nodded to the table to an extra pair of 3D goggles.

"I would, but I think it best we head upstairs. And the gift...open it later."

I agreed, and we left the room. Ezra took the service elevator, and I climbed the stairs as was my usual, having a strong distaste for the wood-box lift.

Both the elevator and the stairs rose to the south wall of the kitchen storage pantries. Mumm's staff was busy—all five women and Mr. Davis Harris, her butler. He was directing their efforts to stage the next entrée. Mumm had hired Mr. Harris three years prior, but it was Father who ordered him about, in contrast to Mumm's suggestions and light requests. Mr. Harris was smiling, and his brow was moist as he nodded, one time, approving of my nonformal attire. Then he tapped his throat to me.

I raised my hand and touched the 3D goggles around my neck. I shrugged, and Mr. Harris winked and led Ezra and me from the kitchen. We walked the parquet to the marbled foyer to the enclosed dining room where music and loud conversations and female laughter were waiting. Mr. Harris rolled the door open, and I stepped into the familiar chaos among the couches and low tables and the bar and dining area.

The long, dark table was set, and the prior entrée had been served. It rested, untouched. The table was beautiful even without the candle-light, due to three fiery accidents in months past. The far glass doors were open to the view and the swimming pool. There were human silhouettes swaying at the water's edge. The glowing blue pool water was an effective backdrop.

Father stood in a half circle of the usual attendees—studio executives, directors, and producers. Most of these men were there on Mumm's behalf, and a few stood off to the side looking displeased with Father and his people. These men were glancing at their wristwatches and the big door waiting for Mumm's entrance.

Ezra was compelled to attend these parties, being a top-notch cameraman, inventor, and engineer, which meant he was a guppy and swam at a constant risk among the employers—the piranhas.

I panned the room and confirmed that Mumm wasn't present. She was partial to the first third of the evenings—the meals and conversation—but usually departed before Father and his friends became, at best, *animated*. If a screening were scheduled or there were dailies to view and critique, Mumm would be on time, staying close to the executives and insulated from Father and his friends.

Ezra circled wide around Father and his crowd. One of the dates—naked, wet, and trembling—came in from the lights and pool and wove through the tuxedos to the fireplace. Mr. Harris offered her a tablecloth, and she stood before the flames shivering and smiling and looking uncertain and dazed. She still wore one of her high heels.

I recognized her as one of Father's constant dates. Her name didn't come to me.

Father was oblivious to her standing in front of the fire and was beckoning with his beefy hand.

"There's my *negro*," he called to Mr. Harris.

Father glanced to his buddies, laughing to himself. Others were turning their heads away, and none of them looked amused. I spotted Mr. Nash with a glass in each hand among those still laughing. He had removed his tuxedo jacket, and his hair was awry.

I panned the partiers, the barely clad dates, the men with their drinks and loosened ties, and the house staff, all of them smiling and nodding and scurrying in response to requests and demands.

I left the doorway to my birthday party and walked up the hall to Mumm's screening room. There was a black velvet curtain between the door and the room, and I parted it and looked in. Rows of fashionable and comfortable chairs descended before the low stage. The tall, black stage curtains were closed. The room was dim—the brightest light coming from the glass popcorn maker to the left of the door. I could smell melted butter, and I took a paper box from the stack. There was no one else in the room, and I took my usual seat in the third row, just off center.

I set my popcorn box on the short table next to my chair. Piano music was playing—a record had been put on in the projector room—and the song carried from the theatre speakers. I pulled on my 3D goggles and ate popcorn and waited.

• • • •

TWENTY MINUTES later, I turned from the stage and watched the doorway curtain part, and Mumm appeared. Mr. Nash held the curtain for her. He left her side and walked to the projector room. Mumm looked resplendent. She wore darling slippers with gold lace appearing below the hem of her sparkling white dress. Her pale skin was just a few shades lighter than the silk. When she saw me, she smiled and walked the decline and sat down beside me. She kept her kind smile to me, framed by her loosely falling blonde-white hair. She took my hand and looked right into my eyes—through her own pair of 3D goggles.

A faint motor hummed, and the stage curtains pulled back into the wings. I listened to the piano music and the chaotic party sounds from down the hall. The noise ebbed and then quickly resumed. I heard clumsy sounds and a curse from the projector room. A white funnel of light cast into the room and haloed Mumm's shoulders and head.

"I believe our Mr. Nash is struggling," Mumm said lightly.

I watched the screen and his efforts to align the images from the dual projectors. I could go and offer to help him, but I didn't. There was another curse, and the needle on the record scratched, and the piano playing stopped.

While the movie screen flickered with test footage, I noticed that the room was still half-dimmed. I got up and worked the sliders on the wall beside the projector room, killing all light.

I took my chair, and Mumm took my hand, and the test footage ended. The film's title resolved from two misaligned images into one, and we were *within* 3-D.

The opening soundtrack was the wind from the sea in the trees. The title, *Savior*, was centered in white dramatic script on the black background.

The credits rolled, and I smiled as each of the members of our film crew was acknowledged. Mr. Nash received multiple credits and the major ones, including "directed by" and "produced by" and, disappointingly to me, "screenplay by." Finally, the screen read, "Based on the short story by BB Danser." I couldn't help a smile.

Our goggles placed each letter, each word, right in our laps, pressing into the skin of our faces. From the corner of my eye, Mumm's outreached hand was touching and petting the credits.

The film began with the view of the meadow and ocean.

There was Mumm, beautiful and tender on-screen and also inside the theatre air resting on our faces and shoulders. I felt a hot flush to my head. I was in the meadow. My hands went out to brush the swaying grass aside so I could see Mumm better. I touched the pale softness of her wrists. I breathed from her as she raised her eyes to the cameras, to me and me only. Her expression was *accepting*.

Mumm breathed deeply in the theatre chair beside mine. I was within the movie and in the movie appearing at her side in the film.

On the screen, there was a rustling of movements behind Mumm as I watched myself move through the grass. The cameras panned and zoomed to my hip and arm.

A voice interrupted the wind in the meadow. It was Mr. Nash cursing from the projector room. I didn't turn, didn't leave the meadow.

There was a significant crash from somewhere else in the mansion. Mumm's hand released mine and gently gripped my knee before she rose from her chair and departed.

The second-to-last scene of *Savior* stopped abruptly, rudely, leaving me with my arms outstretched as hot, flickering blue and yellow light replaced the story on the screen.

"That's it for now, boy-o," Mr. Nash called through the projector window.

A moment later, the theatre lights were raised, and the screen went white.

I heard men's voices from behind and kept my goggles on and aimed at the dull movie screen. The stage curtains slid to a close as the door to the screening room opened and loud voices—Father's especially—entered.

He staggered in with the hands of others grasping for his tuxedo. The hands missed, and he parted the black door curtain with his gaggle of friends and their heated voices, some pleading with Father and others encouraging. The clamor of red faces and hands and disheveled tuxedos stumbled into the room. The popcorn machine was toppled and hit the ground with a spray of glass and popped kernels. Father stepped to the front of the group with his finger pointed at me.

"Boy! So it's *your* day. Get up on the stage."

I stared.

"Now, dimwit!"

I stood. The guests were panning out, both the men and their dates. I heard Ezra's voice pleading ineffectively in the mix. I walked down to the base of the stage.

"Curtains!" Father bellowed.

The stage curtains parted as I climbed up onto the planks of the stage.

"Lights!"

The projectors were turned on and washed me, blinded me. I could no longer see anyone or the room, just that hot and brilliant beam.

This had happened before. In fact, this had happened every birthday that I could recall.

"Music!"

A new record was put on. Gypsy music began from the many speakers—an odd and uncertain rhythm and melody I had heard and hated for years. I stood facing the light, feeling the heat it was giving off.

"Take off those stupid goggles!" Father commanded. "A jig for your master's pleasure!"

Mumm's voice entered the chaos, sharp and cutting, taking up my defense along with Ezra.

Father ignored them and barked, "Boy. Dance!"

"*IM. Stop!*" Mumm yelled, bravely.

I didn't remove my goggles, but I began to sway my shoulders and arms, hesitantly, in the heat from the projector lamp and my humiliation.

"Dance for your cake!" Father roared.

Hands began to clap in rhythm and voices continued to both encourage and contest this scene. I danced on the planks. When Father demanded, "Loosen up!" I did my best, knowing well of the fast fists and kicking I'd receive if I didn't please. Not right away, not with Mumm and the guests present, but late in the night or near dawn. While the rest of the mansion slept, he'd awaken, like a rabid bear from hibernation in search of mayhem—to appease his hunger, to feed his knuckles.

I heard a scuffle begin that I couldn't see and alarmed voices yelling. I heard Mumm's stage name called out. The music was cut. There was grappling and curses as a fight started. The projector was killed, and I stopped dancing.

"You drunken fool!" Mumm yelled.

"No one's gonna talk to me like that!" he hollered back, followed by the sound of a punch.

I pulled my goggles to my neck and saw Mumm on the floor, Ezra beside her. The gaggle parted, and Mr. Nash shoved Father back through the curtain. He had hit Mumm in the face.

From out in the foyer, the sounds of a brawl began. I jumped down from the stage and ran to Mumm. Ezra was helping her to her feet when I reached her. She looked both dazed and focused, and the left side of her face was red, the beginning of a bruise.

"I'm fine, love," she said to me, ignoring the others trying to assist her.

Ezra had his arm around her, and I took her other side. One of the tallest men parted the curtain, and we left the screening room, a studio executive leading the way. We stayed close to Mumm as we entered the foyer.

Dates were crying and calling out as we circled the border of the brawl. Mr. Harris was in the thick of the fight trying to divide the two teams like a referee. Father was outnumbered—he had two remaining allies, beefy and stupid-looking men, once famous actors. Mumm and our group finished our wide circling to the main staircase. Two of the kitchen staff met up with us, one holding a cloth full of ice. I saw Mr. Nash swing a round-the-barn fist at Father's head. Father ducked to the side and wasn't hit. Father planted his shoe hard up into Mr. Nash's crotch. Mr. Nash went down as we started up the stairs.

Halfway up along the curve, I looked down into the fight. Father had broken free and was over at the front doors bellowing in rage. He spun back into the room swinging a cane from the umbrella stand. I continued upward as he began to change the tide of the battle to his advantage.

The dates continued screaming, fists and feet were swinging, furniture was upended. At the top of the stairs, I witnessed Mr. Harris end the brawl by smashing a vase against the back of Father's head. IM inelegantly crumbled to the marble floor.

"Her face, you moron!" was the final shout by Mr. Nash, who followed his words by kicking the side of Father's prone head.

I followed Mumm and Ezra and the others inside the sitting room of Mumm's suite. Only Ezra was speaking, somewhat of a rant, that Mumm ended by saying to him, "Darling, please, hush." I paused my nodding head to his chatter, noting the *darling*.

The tall men remained at the door guarding it and talking softly. I heard them speaking of Mumm's invaluable face and glowing career and Father's clattering downhill slide.

"His is in the rubble," one of them said.

The clamor downstairs ended, settling back to earth like spiraling dust sinking to the marble floor. Ezra was beckoned to the couch where he sat down beside Mumm, and she took his hand. She held the cloth of ice in her other hand at the side of her face. I stood in the cluster of staff and protectors. Mumm looked up at me, so beautiful and so weary, an expression like a bear in the zoo.

The last words she said to me were, "Go save her."

• • • •

INSTEAD OF going to my bedroom there on the second floor, I went downstairs to the lab. I selected a freshly laundered blanket and a pillow from a shelf and lay down on the couch. A deadened sleep came surprisingly fast but was interrupted by brief explosions of voices and footsteps carrying from the air vents. These sounds snuck into my ears and became the soundtrack of my manic dreams.

In the wee hours, the creaking of the descending elevator woke me. I raised my head from within my blanket and stretched my eyes open wide when I heard a key in the door lock. The only light in the lab was from a standing lamp in the far corner. Its glow almost reached the door, which creaked open to reveal Father. The light was too faint to illuminate my seven mirrors, so I watched Father cross to my tables in a singular view. It seemed that another person was in the doorway, undefinable and silent in the shadows.

Father began shuffling through my books and magazines, disrupting the orderly stacks. I saw that my writing pad was closed and hoped he wouldn't explore my satchel, which was there on the table.

He hadn't looked to me—perhaps he thought I was still asleep. He read and muttered the titles of a few of my dime novels, my collection of *Weird Stories*, my H. P. Lovecraft collection, and my *Argosy* and *True Detectives* magazines. He found my copies of *Spicy Detectives* at the bottom of the stack and snorted—his style of laughter. He breathed the words, "Naughty boy," and turned and looked at me.

I sat up and swung my blanket to the side.

"Would you like to see some real smut, boy? I've got a film, a few films, of your Mumm, as you call her, *entertaining* herself. Up there in her big, beautiful bed. Ever seen your Mumm naked? All shivering and un-done? And boy, can she get on a naughty mouth when she's in a lather."

I watched him look away at the door.

"I have my own mirrors," he continued. "Two-way mirrors. And my bedroom's right next to hers. Just like what they do in your smutty detective books and magazines."

Father turned and faced me. A smile stretched his face.

"I offered her a solution. A *pact*, if you know what I mean."

I didn't. The word reminded me of *agreement* and *contract* and what I had read about suicide pacts. I didn't ask him to clarify. I watched him sit on the table and begin to swing his legs, childlike.

"She declined," he said in the softest, calmest version of his voice I was ever to hear.

"We've been gone," he continued, changing tact with barely a pause. "Traveling for hours. You and I."

I had no idea what he was talking about.

"The accident upstairs occurred while we arrived at the train station."

I blinked my eyes tight at the word *accident* and stared at his throat.

"Now get dressed," he spat out, his voice again deep and controlling, directing.

"And stop that," he said, mimicking the nodding and turning of my head from side to side along the row of his words.

"Get to the car," he ordered.

I stood from the couch. Father pointed to my shoes on the rug. I was awake but also groggy and not cautious, and I braved, "Is Mumm okay?"

He actually growled from low in his throat. I looked away to the door between my mirrors. There *was* a person standing there in his shadow. I saw that it was a woman.

He stood from my table and left the room with the woman in tow. I pulled on my clothes and vest and my coat from the back of the couch.

I opened my satchel and slid my writing pad and letters inside. I saw the birthday gift from Ezra and put it in as well.

When I entered the kitchen from the stairs, Father and his familiar-looking date stood outside the open mouth of the elevator. The room was dark and quiet. The last time I had spied her, she was coming in from the swimming pool naked.

The door to the carport was open. The headlights of Mumm's car were shining across the driveway. Father saw what I was going to do before I had even decided. I spun from them and the doorway, turning to the other door, to the foyer, the stairs, to Mumm's room, to Mumm.

He swung fast and hard, and I believe it was a tall redwood pepper shaker that he clobbered me with, fading me to black and putting an end to my attempted rescue.

ACT TWO
WILDWOOD

Save

To make safe; to procure the safety of; to preserve from injury, destruction, or evil of any kind; to rescue from impending danger; as, to save a house from the flames

<u>Scene 3</u>

I spent the five days on the train slumped in my seat beside the window with the blinds drawn. The headaches wouldn't allow me to move, and I threw up constantly. When I opened my eyes, part of my vision was clear and other areas were unfocused. I had the compartment to myself, and from time to time a steward brought me sandwiches, colas, bags of ice for the wound on my head, and clean buckets to vomit in.

We spent four days in Ann Arbor, Father's hometown. I believe he had family there, but we stayed at a low-profile motel on the outskirts of the city. On the morning of our last day there, a doctor arrived. An area on the back of my head was shaved and sutured. By that time, my vision was almost clear except for faces. I couldn't see eyes, only the shapes of heads, the centered noses, and expressive mouths.

Father told me to drive the hired car. Up front, I had my satchel and a motel towel rolled behind my neck. He was reclining in the back seat with his briefcase, and with Heidi, who Father preferred to call Heidi Ho.

"As in h-o-l-e," he explained with his snorting laugh.

"Heidi Ho!" he called out like a boisterous greeting.

Heidi Ho protested.

He cupped her knee in his big, strong hand and said, "Darling, shut up."

The roads going north were paved for a while and then became gravel. Snow was falling, and I drove as slowly as possible without getting an earful from Father. We were on what he called the parallels. I had no idea what he meant.

The turn-off to his family's summer cottage didn't have a name.

"Turn here, boy. It's our road."

I did, and from then on, the twisty dirt road was known as Our Road. Our Road loosely paralleled a lake as it wove through the trees along many tight turns.

"Burnin' the clutch, boy," I heard four times along those two twisting miles to the cottage.

The little house was on the lake and had a dock and but no electricity inside. Father spent two hours out in the snow with a ladder and ran a drop to the cottage, stealing electricity from the strand of poles that led to the wealthy, year-round, large homes on the east side of the lake. Huddled on the short couch, I listened to him tell Heidi Ho about the parties at those fine houses—the ones he used to be invited to.

All this snow and country was new to me having spent all my life in Inglewood, ten miles from where he and Mumm worked in Hollywood. I asked, once, why we were at the summer cottage in winter.

"Shut your pie hole."

In Ann Arbor, I had called the mansion—no answer. I also tried to buy a newspaper in the motel office to see what news there was about

Mumm, but I was struggling, throwing up a lot, and moving slow. Father spotted me, hooked my elbow, and turned me around.

"Guess I cracked your egg. Behave, or I'll scramble it."

• • • •

THAT FIRST day at the cottage we had the single light from a bulb in the narrow kitchen, but no heat. Heidi Ho found two oil lanterns on a shelf and lit them with the box of stove matches. She tore a yellowed newspaper into strips and told me to put them in my shoes for warmth. I did.

I spent the late afternoon curled on the short couch, sometimes shivering, even though Heidi Ho had found a thin blanket for me. I searched the pantry and found a tin of saltines. After eating all of them, I decided to keep the tin. I placed the Luscious letters inside and buried the tin at the bottom of my satchel.

It was quiet and cold, and they were upstairs in the loft where they rhythmically bounced. Dust fell from the ceiling boards above me.

I stayed on the couch facing the lake-view window. Even with the strips of newspaper in my shoes, my feet were freezing, and I found it helpful to rub my toes together. I took out my View-Master as the sun glowed through cloud openings and used its light to illuminate my reels of 3D images. I don't know why, but within the View-Master, faces were clear and focused, and I could see all the details of eyes.

The sun disappeared in the background of *World War II Heroes*. I moved an oil lantern to the windowsill as the last of the day's light sank into the frozen lake. It began to snow.

In the middle of the night, I listened to Heidi Ho tiptoe down the narrow stairs and pour a glass of water at the tap. She must have seen me sit up because she offered me ice wrapped in a rag which I declined. She went up the stairs, and I curled back up on the short couch with my shoes still on under the thin blanket.

I was awakened before the dawn's light by Father shouting down from the loft.

"Boy! Go and get my briefcase from the car!"

It was snowing, and my shoes and pant legs were wet when I returned from the auto. Heidi Ho was downstairs and took the briefcase from me without a word. I noted that her lips were void of lipstick and tried to envision her eyes before she climbed to the loft. I sat on the couch wishing that I hadn't eaten all the saltines the day before.

The western sky lightened into a gray sweep over the flat silver lake. I could hear Father's voice from time to time. He was speaking oddly, fast and repetitive, and I distinctly heard him say, "I've shed my skin, but I'm still a snake." It was clear that he was working himself into a lather while Heidi Ho cooed, trying to sedate him.

She came down the steep wooden stairs after an hour of Father's strange talk.

"He gave me cash. We're to go to town for food and clothes. And more lanterns," she explained.

I set my View-Master down with regret. I had been studying the eyes of famous men in *American Presidents*.

Once I got the automobile backed out, the drive was easy but slow. The snow was bumper deep. Heidi sat in the back with the cash. The little town of Wildwood had grand and tall buildings and homes with wrap-around porches and wide, graceful front steps. Most of these structures were shuttered, and many long driveways led to empty lots of rubble. I suppose that the town had at one time seen its heyday, but the buildings and houses stood like weathered ghosts facing the frozen lake.

The grocery store was in the middle of town, and we parked right at the door—the lot was barren save for two snow-covered, rusted sedans. Heidi was pleased to discover that the place was more of a general store. In addition to food and lanterns, there were two shelves of clothing and a hanging rack of shirts, coats, and dresses.

On the drive back to the cottage, Heidi held a newspaper in shaky hands. At one point she said to herself, "I'm kicking it."

I had no idea what she was talking about. I focused on keeping the auto on the ill-defined, twisting road. When I braved a glance into the rearview mirror, her lips were sounding out the words below her pert nose and missing eyes. I was hoping that seeing eyes again would return even if it included Father's dark and baggy ones.

At the cottage, Heidi carried the clothing inside, and I made two trips to bring in the cardboard boxes of food and lanterns. As I unpacked the groceries, Heidi fueled the new lanterns but didn't light them. She placed them back inside a box and carried them out through the front door without explanation.

I took to my couch and, under the thin blanket, changed all my clothing save my vest. Looking out the lake window, I studied the dock. The one piece of clothing I had asked for at the store was a gray coat, and I pulled it on as I studied the line of white crusted boards extending out over the frozen water.

I was drawn out to the dock. Kicking snow off the boards, I walked out to its end. The ice on the lake looked like cellophane. Somewhere far under the ice, fish lived, and I wondered how.

There was a party over on the property farther along the east side of the lakeshore. Their place was a hundred yards away around the curve of the lake. It had electricity, lots of it like we had in Inglewood, and their many windows and doors were lit. I looked back up the dock to the narrow cottage and the single bulb in the open back door.

There was a group of eight men constructing something out on the ice on the lake, a bunch of fellows walking back and forth stacking and arranging. Some added furniture to the mound and others stacked and leaned timber.

Father's voice began booming, like artillery, and Heidi joined the fracas, her voice panicked and pleading, her tone crisp and much higher than his.

I walked back up the dock to the shore and went inside. Father was still upstairs, but his ranting and cursing carried down those steep and narrow stairs. Heidi climbed down, her mouth quivering, her nose red and moist. She was carrying a shovel, and I watched her go out the front door with it.

She was gone—out in the cold—for a good two hours. During that time, I View-Mastered faces with eyes and thought about those men building that haphazard structure out on the ice.

When the sun began to set, I found a rusty can opener and ate a can of cold corn. Heidi came back inside, her clothing filthy with soil stains and her cheeks and hands smudged with dirt. She was shivering and cursing and stood at the sink where she washed up quickly. I watched her strip to her undies and pull on a pair of men's tan corduroys and a checkered flannel shirt. I didn't speak, and neither did she—not to me, anyway. She talked to herself under her breath, saying things I didn't understand. All I caught was Father's name over and over, "IM, IM..."

When she had climbed the stairs to Father's voice, I listened for ten minutes trying to figure out what they were discussing. All I could hear was harsh whispering. I buttoned up my new gray coat and went out to the lake.

The sky was clear, and the sunset was a sideways explosion of gold and burgundy. I turned to the big home and the party and the structure on the ice. I could hear music and an occasional loud laugh carrying from the well-lit crowd on the patio and the gentle sloping, snow-covered lawn.

When darkness fell, a man carrying a red-glowing road flare started the fire on the lake. I assumed that gasoline or lantern oil had been poured because the bonfire rose fast. Standing in a clearing along the shore about halfway to the party, I watched the flames weave up through the furniture and timber, pouring black smoke upward. People were applauding and calling out to each other and laughing. Their voices carried over to me like false heat from the fire that I couldn't feel but was nonetheless warmed by. I entered the tree line and followed the curve of the shore to the gathering.

Twenty yards from the big house, I thought I could feel the heat from the flames, but maybe not. Men and women and a few children were moving in the glow of the bonfire and the large lit windows and patio doors. Three men walked down the white lawn and out onto the lake to a structure of tubes and equipment. I watched them in the flickering light as they knelt and talked and worked.

"Hey," a child's voice called to me. "Wanna play?"

To my right, I saw a boy of about eight watching me over a low hedge.

"We're celebrating daylight saving time ending," he explained.

I looked back along the shore to our place. I was worried. Father had a really bad temper when he found me out of earshot. The boy was smiling and held a barbecued turkey leg in his hand. My thoughts of Father made that low hedge appear to rise.

The first firework launched from a tube with a gritty rush of wind and a gray tail following it into the black sky. It rose hundreds of feet and exploded in brilliant gold crystals. Those gathered on the patio and the lawn were shouting with delight and amazement, and another firework was launched with the same rushing sound, blasting glittering green sparks high, high above.

"Well?" the boy asked.

A million green stars were falling from above and blinking out before they reached land.

"We have lots to eat."

I was hungry and fearful of Father finding me gone. When the boy took a hearty bite from the turkey leg, I climbed over the hedge.

I stayed on the perimeter of the festive crowd to the side and out of the direct light. Two other children, about the boy's age, joined him, and I noticed him losing interest in me. The other two were lovely, chatting girls. Up above, two fireworks exploded at the same time, and we were all bathed in a blend of purple and yellow.

"Hungry?" the boy asked.

Without looking down to him, I answered, "Yes. Please."

He walked up the lawn and entered the house. Through the tall, lake-view windows, he moved along the buffet set up in the warmly lit interior. I waded further into the crowd with their heads tilted back to watch the exploding sky, and I stood directly in between the bonfire and the house. Music was wavering from the home.

"No!" A man screamed from the lake.

I turned.

Out on the ice, he fell back, rolled, and scrambled to the row of tubes. A rocket launched, and the firework took off horizontally instead of skyward. A second later, a blue cascade of sparks exploded against the left wall of the house beside the double doors. People were yelling and ducking in the blue glow.

The boy walked through the doors with a plate in his hands.

Two men yelled from the lake, and I turned to them.

Despite their efforts, a second rocket took off. It skimmed like a missile and struck a lounge chair and dining table on the patio with a hot, silver, glittering explosion that sprayed the nearby partiers. There was screaming from the man at the tubes and the crowd as people ducked and hid. The only persons standing were the boy with the two girls holding plates with their jaws dropped.

I broke into a run.

Another rocket launched.

I began to shout as I ran, planning to tackle or knock him down.

"Get down! Get down!" I yelled.

Halfway to the boy, I tripped over a sprinkler head buried in the snow.

I fell, plowing snow into my face.

There was an explosion of orange against the second story of the house, and I rolled to my feet and ran for boy, screaming at him.

The next missile struck him square in the chest. He was slammed from his feet backward in through the doorway. His body was a silver hurricane of sparks and bright light and flying, burning goo.

The two girls were also hit and went down spinning and screaming. I ran across the patio, past huddling, kneeling guests, and toppled furniture.

I reached the boy. He was in flames, arms flailing, screeching in agony. A man braved the flames and climbed over the boy, hands pounding. Another tossed in a tablecloth, and the man and boy rolled. The tablecloth caught fire in the arcing spray of flame and silver. The man's clothing caught fire, but he kept pounding the boy's body and the spewing, bright molten flame.

I was knocked down, and I knelt on the patio bricks where I watched men and women swarm the boy and the two girls with water and tablecloths. The boy stopped screaming before the fire on him was extinguished.

I knelt there in the chaos. My attempt to save him had failed. The dinner plate that the boy had been bringing me was upside down on the patio, and I stared at it while the two girls and others screamed and cried out.

The smell was ghastly—hot phosphorous and burning, boiling flesh.

•　•　•　•

A HALF-HOUR later, an ambulance arrived from the city, and the bonfire had weakened to just below head height. All the people had moved inside, and I could see them through the windows. The patio was scattered with overturned furniture and discarded paper plates and cups. I stood up so I could watch the ambulance driver in the crowd. He and his partner were on their knees with an open medical box working frantically to save those two little girls.

When the ambulance headed off into the night, I walked to the big window and put my hands on the glass. The scene inside was full of grief and sadness. A fight broke out among three of the men, and I stood in the snow watching the brawl of fists and kicks until it ended.

Eventually, the partygoers thinned out, and I turned away. The bonfire was at a low ebb. Across the curve of the lake that single light bulb lit the cottage. I climbed over the low hedge and entered the trees and brush making my way back.

The cottage was silent. I stood still just inside the lake door for five minutes with my ears expectant and aimed to the loft. No creaking ceiling boards, no voices.

I wondered if Father and Heidi had found sleep. I noticed that the front door was open because a cold draft was crossing to me. Instead of climbing the stairs for a peek, I walked to the front door and out through it, closing it behind me.

I walked along the side of the windowless wall. When I turned the corner of the house, I saw lantern light out in the trees. Four had been lit and set out in a rectangle behind wooden frames draped with white sheets. The structures of thin linen glowed from within. A single, low silhouette of a head and shoulders rocked side to side.

I walked closer and paused with my hand on the front curtain.

Father was ranting but doing so low and softly. Heidi was sobbing.

"Must be a better solution," she tried, her voice wet with tears.

"We have our pact, our agreement," he replied, deep and sure.

I parted the linen and looked inside.

There was a pit surrounded by lanterns.

Father stood in the hole, his clothing slicked with mud and his fedora and shoulders white with fresh snow.

"There's our dimwitted third wheel," he spotted me.

"Sit, boy," he demanded.

I did on the dirt mound beside a shovel. My butt wanted to slide until I planted my paper-filled shoes, heels first. Heidi sat on the edge of the hole, arms locked across her chest. Father gave her a *come here* gesture with his big hand. She stopped crying.

She slid down, mucking up her shoes, clothing, and handbag. She stood beside him and his briefcase and a shotgun I hadn't noticed before.

The snow was falling harder. They both looked tan in the lantern light. Heidi had changed into her travel dress and held her purse in both hands. Her head was turning from Father's to me. I watched Father's nose and mouth. He was offering a stream of gibberish which he broke off.

"Boy. Welcome to our big finale. This will unite us all. Climb down here. Onto the stage, so to..."

He didn't finish. I slid down the wall of snow and mud into the shallow pit that was wide enough to bury a piano in. I pressed my back against the wall facing Father and Heidi, who stood by his side.

"Good, boy. Say that you admire this well-lighted theatre."

I did.

He offered Heidi the shotgun, and she took it after setting her purse on the snow and mud at her feet.

"What happened to Mumm?" I braved. I watched his wide lips pinch and his jaw chew to the side.

"Her? Yes, we could offer a prayer for her...her beautiful face and slutty ways, but no. She departed earlier. Whisked right off the stage and into the wings."

I tried to make sense of that. He interrupted me. "Boy, stop that. Moving your head like some godforsaken typewriter."

I stopped the sweeping nod I was tracing and searching his words with.

"I'm packed and ready to go," he went on, his hands twisting on the handle of his briefcase. "Miss Ho will leave first. Then you. I'll depart last. This is my movie, so I get the very last scene."

"I've kicked the horse and tar," she was hesitating, teeth chattering. "Doesn't have to go this way."

Father turned slowly to her, head tilted to one side.

"So? Your future is nothing. Bent over, being pumped by strangers until you're a hag."

Heidi got an elbow to the ribs and coughed in pain. She tilted the barrel of the shotgun toward her face and began to cry again.

Father struck her hard with the back of his hand, and she yelped, and he reached out to me. His big hand opened, and I saw a shotgun cartridge. He nodded toward the rifle in Heidi's hands and explained, "It only holds two. I get this one."

I looked to Heidi with the barrel before her mouth.

"Miss Ho, do as scripted. Hit your marks."

Heidi's hands were shaking. She adjusted the length of the shotgun and placed the barrel between her lips and slid it in an inch.

"Oh. Pause," Father said, "I do love that image. Okay, and thank you. It's a picture I'll lovingly take to...well, you know."

"I forgot my satchel," I said, hoping to break the spell of madness, a reason to climb out of the pit.

"No matter," Father said.

He turned from her and locked his hand on my arm and tugged. My feet tangled on themselves in the snow and mud.

I hit my knees.

He cocked his fist to knock me lower.

Heidi pulled one of the triggers.

After sliding the barrel from her mouth and aiming it at Father's face.

• • • •

FATHER'S BLOOD and hat and hair and brains splattered against the top edge of the grave. The fresh snow and the draped, white linens were splashed with his blood.

"Boy," Heidi said, her voice shaking, "save this." She kicked Father's briefcase across to me in the wet muck.

I watched her struggle to climb out of the hole, hands trembling, but determined. After a slip, she clawed her way up and out and stood there in her filthy dress.

"I'm gonna go change." Her head was swinging wildly side to side. "Clean myself up. You get to work."

"What?"

"Fill the grave, dimwit."

I climbed out and took up the shovel. Father had been blown back and lay with one knee up. I paused, staring at what remained of him. And the end of my torment.

The first shovel of dirt landed on his missing face and ripped-open throat.

The second shovelful covered more of that bloody mess and reminder. After that, I went to work in earnest.

I was nearly done filling the grave when Heidi came out and took down the lighting panels and boxed up the extinguished lanterns. Fifteen minutes later, we stood side by side. She was studying my handiwork. I was watching falling snow covering the mound.

"Where's the briefcase?" she asked, breaking the silence.

"With Father."

"You moron. Dig it out. We need cash."

I turned to her. Clean clothed, fresh makeup, but looking and sounding twitchy.

"I took some." I hoped that would help.

"How much?" her teeth chattered.

"Three packets."

"Hmm." She breathed deeply. "That should do. Give 'em to me."

I gave the packets to her, and they went inside her purse. Earlier, I had pocketed one for myself.

Heidi told me to unplug the borrowed electricity, and I did.

"I would have liked to see his eyes before the end," I said to her.

"Your father's? They were full of disappointment. And surprise."

"No. The boy's."

"Who? What boy?"

"Like Father says. *Said.* No matter."

Heidi gripped her purse close, and I shouldered my satchel, and we closed up the cottage and walked out to the snow-covered automobile.

Scene 4

We entered the Grand Belle Tower Hotel at 2:00 a.m. Crossing the clean, warm lobby, I was keenly aware of my filthy clothing. In particular, my mud-caked shoes on the gold carpeting. The soft-spoken woman at the registration desk paid no mind to my appearance. Heidi selected the suggested parlor suite and paid cash up front.

I kicked off my shoes just inside the door to our suite, and Heidi walked to the second room, leaving crusts of snow and dirt and discarded clothing in her wake. When she stopped at the foot of the bed, she was naked to her undies and carrying her purse in one hand. I sat on the carpet instead of muddying up a chair or the couch. I was getting one of the bad headaches like I had on the train.

The misting sound of Heidi's shower was interrupted by a knock on the door. I opened it to a sleepy, ferret-faced man in a Belle Tower vest who went into the bedroom and turned down the single large bed. He came into the front room and lit the fireplace with wooden matches from the mantel. I got up from the carpet and offered him a tip from my cash packet. He refused it, smiled, and left.

I saw Heidi fresh from the shower and naked for the second time in a handful of days. She had a towel wrapped around her hair and sat on the couch, facing the fire. She picked up the telephone receiver from the end table. I went into the bedroom and retrieved one of the two folded robes from the foot of the bed and brought it to her. She stood and stretched backward while talking on the phone. I listened to her ask the front desk about purchasing clothes—it seemed that the hour of the night was a problem.

She hung up, pulled on the robe, and sat on the couch and looked to me.

"Boy. Push your eyeballs back in and go clean yourself up. I'll see if the kitchen is open."

I headed off to bathe while she placed the second call.

I took my time in the shower tub. I watched dirt slide from my skin and form a swirling pool of brown water at the drain hole. Warm water on my face seemed to help reduce the headache. Swimming clouds of dried and dissolved blood were swirling around my feet. I realized I had been splattered when Father was killed. I briefly wondered if the night clerk had called the police. Then I found the soap bar and that question dissolved as I washed my face.

When I left the bathroom, I pulled on the second robe and gathered up my clothing and pushed them inside a laundry bag. I followed the path of Heidi's clothing.

She was seated at the dining cart that had been wheeled in during my absence. There was enough food and drinks for five on the nicely set table, and I realized how hungry I was. We sat across from each other and started in on the selection of breakfast and dinner entrees.

"He'd been hunting for one like me," she said as she took a sip of coffee.

I set my fork down.

"Hunting?" I asked.

"*I need a hand to hold, to take along.*" She did a fair imitation of his gruff voice. "*You've got nothing to live for.*"

"That isn't true, right?" I asked.

"He thought so. My profession. The drugs."

I looked straight across the table wishing I could again see people's eyes—*her* eyes. There was nothing but blurring above her attractive nose.

"He only got three things wrong," she continued.

"Yes?"

"One, thinking my life was worthless. Two, believing if I were going to heaven, I'd go with him."

"And?"

"Handing me the shotgun."

•   •   •   •

WE FINISHED the meal in silence. The clock on the mantle read 4:00 a.m. Heidi told me to get rid of the table, and I wheeled it out into the hall. I came back inside and saw that she had left the front room, and the bedroom door was closed. I found a blanket in the short hall closet and lay on the couch. I watched the fire and felt the headache dissolving as I melted toward sleep.

I was about to close my eyes when Heidi called out, "Boy. How old are you?"

I sat up and turned to the bedroom door.

"Fifteen," I called back to her.

"Come here. I want to taste you."

Scene 5

When I woke, the bedroom windows were bright with midday light. Heidi was gone from the bed, and while I couldn't hear her voice, I did hear the rustling of paper and cardboard. I found my robe entangled in the bedding and pulled it on and went out to the front room. Heidi was standing in front of the couch before a row of shopping bags and shoeboxes. She had pulled on undies and a bra.

"Your pile's over there," she told me, not turning, but pointing to the loveseat to the side.

Half awake, I was swirling with images of her body and what we had done in that big bed.

Her back remained to me.

"Get with it, boy," she instructed.

I crossed the carpet and opened clothing bags and boxes searching for underwear first.

We ate a silent, late lunch in the restaurant downstairs, both of us freshly attired in loose fitting and dark-colored clothes for travel.

Like Father, Heidi didn't care that I wasn't legally old enough to drive. She told me to get the car from the lot and meet her in front of the hotel. When she came out through the lobby doors held open by a man in a Belle Tower vest, she only carried her purse. I assumed she had rented the suite for another night because all our other new clothing was up there. She surprised me by circling the automobile to my door.

"Scoot," she told me, and I did.

Heidi got in behind the wheel and steered us deeper into Ann Arbor. She stopped once to ask for directions at a service station where she also had the tank filled and the windshield sprayed and wiped.

"We're going to sell the car," she said, applying apple red lipstick and watching the service attendant. "Might as well have it looking good to get the most."

I nodded. I was headache free. I didn't understand how we could sell a hired car. I found it odd that making the auto *look good* didn't include washing the hem of dust and mud from all four sides. I didn't ask.

The parking lot at the train depot was full of automobiles, but there were only a few travelers to see. Heidi parked at the curb and slid a twenty from a packet in her purse. She handed it to me and said, "Go get us a train schedule. And a newspaper. Maybe there's something about your mother."

It was way too much money for a newspaper, but there weren't any smaller bills. I climbed the walkway that was shiny and wet with shoveled snow to the sides. I went through the tall glass doors and spotted the ticket booth. The woman behind the counter didn't raise her mouth or nose but pointed out her window to a box of folded schedules. I took one.

Like the front of the depot, the interior was empty. High, green glass walls rose three stories before coving to the ceiling. I walked to the snack bar, but it was shuttered and had a sign hanging on the grilled door: "Back at 4:30."

To the side was a newspaper box. I bent to look at the headlines and saw that the box was empty.

I walked back across the lobby full of pale green light and out into the afternoon sky. My satchel was on the curb, and our automobile and Heidi were gone.

Scene 6

Under the green window light, I sat on a wooden bench and looked through the train schedule. When the big display clock read 4:15 p.m., a train entered the depot. Within a minute, the cavernous station was filled with footsteps and voices. A crowd of people washed in like a wave that left echoes as the water receded. I recalled the few times Mumm and I had taken an *idyllic* to the beach, she with her umbrella and me in the surf.

I had the long, wooden bench all to myself and opened my satchel on it. Unfolding my map of California, I traced the lines of crosses that showed train tracks to the west. I saw that a line neared the town of Greenland within a half-inch. While I was missing maps for the other states across America, I was encouraged. I went to the snack bar and broke the twenty for a candy bar and a bottle of cola. The news box had been restocked. I used the change to buy a newspaper and carried it to my bench.

Searching page by page, I scanned for Elizabeth Stark, Mumm's actress name. Her name appeared on the society and gossip page along with a grainy publicity photo. The image was twice as large as the single column article that was titled, "Vanished?"

The first two paragraphs used the words *rumored, speculation,* and *whispered* without any facts, but lots of suggestions, mostly with exclamation marks. The article was suspicious of a studio press release stating that the current film she was on had been halted: "While Ms. Stark crossed the Atlantic to be at her brother's deathbed." The paper offered steamy suspicions that wove in her husband's wild parties and recent brawls and his own disappearance. I was equally suspicious because I knew that Mumm, like me, was an only child. The remainder of the article was a scolding of Hollywood for its decadence and closed with a parable about greed and sin.

Taking all the coins from my pocket, I crossed the green cavern to the row of phone booths. Sitting down and closing the door, I dialed Ezra's number. Neither he nor his secretary picked up. The next call was to the mansion. The telephone rang and rang eight or nine times before I ended the call. My third call was to Mumm's message service.

The operator knew me by voice and shared that Mumm had seventeen unanswered messages.

"When she calls in for them, can you ask her to leave me a message?" I asked. "I need to know that she is safe. I'll call in again in two days."

"I sure will, and you ignore the nonsense in the newspapers."

Either way, I was headed west. If I received a message from Mumm, I could always change direction.

I walked to the ticket window and bought passage to the town nearest Greenland. I did so, recalling Mumm's last words to me, her request: "Go save her."

• • • •

THE SLEEPER compartment had two double seats facing one another under the window and a bed that folded up to the ceiling. There was a short couch that looked like it could be made into a second bed. The door slid open, and a porter introduced himself.

"Please call me George." His nose and mouth cringed at the name before he offered a professional smile.

George showed me the narrow bathroom inside a click-lock door and asked if I had checked any luggage.

"I don't have any."

"Don't hesitate to let me know if you need anything."

"Thank you."

When he turned to leave, there was a knock on the side of the sliding door. I was sitting on the double seat facing west when a very tall and thin man stepped inside. George referenced a clipboard and introduced Mr. Wysan Grub to me. I noticed that Mr. Grub wore a nice vest similar to mine. He removed his great coat and hung it on a hook. George left, and Mr. Grub turned to me.

"Looks like we're sharing the berth. I'm assigned the less expensive upper bed. Call me Wysan, please."

I introduced myself and studied his twitchy smile after he closed our door.

The train departed. An hour later, Wysan Grub and I ate in the dining car at separate tables. He had asked to join me, but a headache was climbing up my neck and into my brain.

"No, I..." Shaking my head was painful.

The train rolled deep into the evening. Later, I listened to him struggle to lower the upper bunk and climb up inside. The train made a few stops in the early night and then ran smoothly for hours. I passed the time with my head covered and my teeth clenched. I awoke at sunrise, not certain if I had slept or not.

Wysan Grub was gone from the compartment most of the day. I alternated between the chair at the window and my bed, napping rather than sleeping. Around sunset, my head had cleared enough to let me eat a meal in the dining car. I found sleep as the sky started to darken.

The sleeper car rattled and slowed as we entered yet another station. I woke up and raised my head. My bedding and the rest of the compartment were blue with moonlight.

Wysan Grub stood in front of my bunk. He held a dripping handkerchief in his hand. His belt and pants were undone. When I looked up at his face, he took a step back. I turned on my bunk light and watched him fumble with the damp cloth and his pants and belt.

"It's the fever," he said in a nervous and shaky voice.

I saw my satchel laying open on the window seat. I climbed out of bed, pushed past him, and grabbed it.

He continued to babble.

"My apologies. The fever..."

He clamored up into his bunk, and I sat against the wall on my bed, the light on, my satchel held close. When he was settled in and had stopped talking, I opened it and did an inventory. Everything was there but had been stirred through. I decided to ring for George and have him get me another compartment.

I was about to close my satchel and get into my clothes when I saw Ezra's gift in the bunk light. I pulled on my pants and my shirt before I opened the package.

Inside was a pair of goggles with a complex of lenses and little levers.

I ignored Mr. Grub. He had restarted his apologetic chatter. Dealing with him had to wait.

I pulled the goggles on.

The world changed.

The view was crisp and immersive, and the compartment was displayed in wondrous layers of 3D. I was looking into a world of hyperrealism—the same vision that Mumm's and my View-Masters provided. I felt my senses expanding, and I tasted a strength, a surety, I had never known. I studied my fingertips in the bunk light. When I exhaled, the world absorbed and embraced my breath. I panned left to right, back and forth, very slowly, my hands touching everything, even the fine details that were out of reach. I felt myself, my world, take on a true and meaningful depth.

I marveled at the changes as I stood up. The amazing solid compartment door opened to the view up the hallway. I walked slowly, panning, absorbing the world. No, *my* world. I walked to the big door at the end of the hall and opened it to wind and cold that I could see as much as feel. Stepping out on the connecting walkway, I looked into the passing countryside. If my life were a puzzle before, it was now complete, and I felt a power, something like being welcomed home.

I stood on the landing watching the chaotic wind and the country-side—a distant rise of hills that I brushed with my fingertips. I didn't hear the door open behind me, and when I felt a hand on my shoulder, I ignored it. I assumed it was George wanting to guide me back inside.

Instead of George, I heard Wysan Grub's voice. "It's freezing, but quite the view."

He was attempting pleasantries. I heard the words and *saw* the undertones. The pretentious chatter was masking his true intentions.

He stepped beside me and nudged my shoulder.

"Crossing the Colorado River!" he yelled into the icy wind.

I ignored that. In my new world, I felt a raw and new decisiveness. And strength.

He turned his face and grinned at me.

And I saw his eyes.

I was able to see eyes again.

His were those of a nervous and deranged wildcat. A predator. A hungry one.

"Watch your footing!" he shouted as he stepped to the rail.

He had that damp rag in his hand again.

In no way did he resemble Father physically, but I *saw* they shared the same cruel mind and dead-heartedness.

I stepped back on the landing and over behind him.

I believe it was my first taste of rage.

My palms struck him full force in the lower back.

He was flung hard into the railing, crying out, his hands scratching for a hold.

I hit him again, and he went over.

After striking the coupling between the cars, he twisted and screamed. Seconds later, the steel wheels ate him. What remained was tossed, broken and splashing, across the trestles and out over the wide and rolling Colorado River.

GREENLAND

Rescue
The act of rescuing; deliverance from restraint, violence, or danger; liberation.

Scene 7

During the rest of the train trip, I spent very little time in the compartment preferring to be around people in the dining, viewing, and reading cars. I knew I was commented on and pointed at because of the goggles, but I ignored that. I focused on the beauty and depth of my new 3D world—a world experienced and seen in breathtaking stereo.

When the train reached the town a half inch away from Greenland on my map, I departed. I slipped away from George's and the conductor's recurring questions about the disappearance of Wysan Grub. Only I knew where Mr. Grub was—arm in arm with Father in hell or wherever evil men landed after death.

I walked into town and entered a hotel. Spotting the phone booths to the left side of the lobby, I called Mumm's answering service. There were no new messages for me. I also learned that she had over twenty-five transcribed messages, all unanswered. Entering the gift shop, I asked the clerk for directions to Greenland.

"Greenland *Homes*? They'll give you a map at the hotel desk, but you can't get there this month...snow and roads."

At the hotel desk, I was offered a room and declined. The woman kept her eyes averted from my goggles and explained, "Fools built Greenland. Them trying to sell homes you can't even get to."

She unfolded a map and drew a circle on a barren area beside what was labeled Starfish Lake.

"Come back in the spring," she told me and asked, "What are you wearing?"

I had my new lie at the ready—the same one used during the last of the train trip.

"Corrective lenses."

She shrugged and suggested I go across the street and buy winter clothes if I was planning to stick around. After declining a room for the second time, I went out onto the road and aligned my new map with the location of the town. A logging truck roared into view, and I stepped to the sidewalk as it passed, its tires sending up a mist of muddy wind that added to the brown mounds of snow in the gutters. A second logging truck passed. I crossed the road as a third appeared in the distance.

The general store had all I needed if not much variety. I changed into new winter clothing and bought a flashlight and a pair of snowshoes, paying from my packet of cash.

I ate lunch in the coffee shop next door. I ordered dinner as well and asked that it be wrapped up. A good number of people gave me odd looks along the lunch counter. I ignored them feeling my new emotion—a mix of confidence and strength.

With the bagged dinner stowed inside my satchel, I walked from the town in the same direction the stream of lumber trucks was coming from. I found it difficult going but safer to trudge along the snow-covered tree line than near the road with those large trucks racing by.

I moved onto the pavement at nightfall when the trucks stopped appearing. Cleaning my goggles constantly, I continued on into my new 3D world, a world of biting cold and falling snow. I didn't check the map in the waning light. I knew I was headed in the right direction.

To Greenland.

To her.

I slept on a bench beside four garbage cans in a roadside shelter. I was woken with a start as the first of the logging trucks roared past. Nearly frozen and dull with hunger, I started out again staying to the safe side of the shoulder, which was hip high and splashed with icy mud.

At midday, I paused long enough to eat the wrapped dinner from the coffee shop.

Two hours later, I stopped again at a Y in the road. The lumber trucks were rolling down the mountain from the right. In the other direction, there was a bridge a hundred yards out and a sign reading "Starfish Lake—5 Miles."

The road to the bridge was deep in snow. There were no vehicle tracks or footmarks. I waited as another truck rounded the long bend, big tires sending up a foul spray. When it was safely past, I started into the thigh-high snow toward the bridge.

Twenty yards out, I stopped and kicked out a small clearing so I could sit down and put on the snowshoes. I stopped again in the middle of the bridge and leaned over the concrete siding. A wild river was tearing downstream between the boulders and rocks.

"Do you feed the Colorado River?" I asked the fast and icy waters rushing the gray stones.

I closed my eyes and pictured dead Wysan Grub floating and bobbing, being carried along to his final place out to sea.

"Flushed. Like garbage down the city drains."

Killing him didn't bother me. I felt no regret or guilt. He had tried to get in my way. It came to me that he was nothing but another obstacle to be rounded or run through.

"I'm on a quest," I said, stealing a recurring line from my comics and detective novels.

"I'm going to save Luscious. And then save Mumm."

• • • •

FIVE MILES isn't that far, even in snowshoes, but I got lost in the hills. It was near nightfall when I came out of the trees and stood before a snowfield that looked a mile long and a mile wide. Off to my left was Starfish Lake.

In the snow silver with moonlight feeling cold and hungry and tired, I took out my flashlight and thumbed the switch.

Within the grasp of my damp mitten, the beam of light raced across the snowfield. The beam dissolved in its reach for the far, northern hill. My stinging ears heard before they felt the next wind off the lake.

The tall trees behind me swayed as a frozen wind slapped my back. The clouds retook the moon while the white beam retreated and, with a small click, disappeared.

I raised my heavy and awkward snowshoe straight up and outward. This snow was different from before—it had a hard crust of ice. My balance was uncertain, and with my knee straight out, the snowshoe rested on the top of the hard, gray pack. I leaned into my knee, and the snowshoe crunched down with resistance at first, then smoothly on further to rest.

Ten tiring strides out, I stopped and again aimed my flashlight to the darkened row of houses on the hill at the far opposite end of the snowfield.

The clouds parted, and the white moon offered an icy light. I felt my empty stomach clench. I watched the great rolling clouds pull together again. When they had, I took another heavy step across the gray snowfield.

I was eighty yards out when I crossed another set of snowshoe footprints. The trail looked like it was cut by kicking, rather than by raise, reach, and push steps. I stopped and worked my mitten into my jacket pocket and removed the flashlight. The tracks were old—not nearly as deep as mine. They appeared to be coming from the far hill and turning there before me to Starfish Lake. I saw that the previous traveler had been weaving and stumbling. I aimed the flashlight to the disrupted snow and recognized bloodstains that, when warm, had burned channels into the white.

I shined the light along the tracks to the east to the lake. I put the flashlight away and continued. A wind full of ice rushed over me burning the back of my neck. I wanted the return of moonlight, but the clouds would not cooperate. I walked in the tracks of the prior traveler which made the going a bit easier, even though the clumsy, blood-stained path wandered left and right.

An hour and a half later, the sky began to lighten with daylight, and I started climbing the hill. I had to concentrate on accurate step placement as I moved upward. I stopped twice and looked up to see the houses, but the brow of the hill blocked my view.

• • • •

WITH THE first light of dawn, I was almost done in—exhausted and nearly frozen. Having finally reached the crest of the steep, relentless hill, my attention was torn. A yellow biplane was slowly banking across the snowfield and distant Starfish Lake at my back. Before me, one of the large houses was going up in flames.

I stood shin deep on a snow-covered lawn between two tall houses. The yellow biplane was angled low above the pines, the sound of its engine wavering in the cold air.

Across the road, orange flames and black smoke boiled through the windows and the open front door. I looked one last time to the airplane, but a dark house blocked my view. I gave my full attention to the burning structure in front of me.

My stomach was no longer growling. Instead, it was cramping. I stared at the fire without a thought of doing anything other than watching. The 3D enlivened black smoke and orange flames were alive and beautifully reflecting on the blue snow. It was the same kind of layered vision Mumm and I had shared with our View-Masters. I could hear the cracking and crashing sounds from inside the house. I knew it wasn't the safest thing to do, but I took a dozen steps closer to warm myself.

Automatic sprinklers came on across the lawns one after another in front of the large houses on both sides of the black-paved road. The thin cones of sprinkler water were turning into ice before they landed.

Something heavy crashed and something crumbled inside the burning house. I watched the drapes in a second-story window ignite. Above, the black smoke was staining the morning sky.

The snowplowed road in front of the burning house was one continuous, sweeping curve. There were no sirens and no adults to be seen. The sun had climbed into the sky high enough to lay strokes of sparkling light on the snow.

I looked to the curb a few feet away thinking I might sit and thaw in the fire's glow. There was a street bench to my left, and I chose it instead. Two strides to it, I stopped. The bench was occupied.

A teenage boy was sitting on the green planks with his shoes and lower pant legs buried in the snow. The arms of his dirty gray jacket were crisscrossed over his chest. He looked roughed up, and there was a paper bag beside him. He was working on half a sandwich held close to his lips. As he chewed, he smiled, his cheekbones raised to the fire for warmth. I was relieved to see another person among the houses with no one else about. I hoped he could help me locate Luscious.

I studied the teen and the remaining half of the sandwich in his filthy hands. I followed his wide-open eyes to the house giving off warmth and crashing sounds. Behind me, the sound of the yellow airplane grew louder. The inside of the teen's dirty jacket began to move, and he restrained it with his arms. I walked across the snow to him.

The airplane was close and loud. I listened to it banking across the face of the hill beneath the Greenland development. After it flew by, the teen took another bite from his sandwich. The fading sound of the airplane was replaced by an automobile coming fast, its motor wound out as far as possible in a low gear.

A power-sliding Cadillac crested the top of the curve, its rear tires spinning. The silver automobile was sideways, its nose aimed at the inside of the turn where its headlights swept the white lawns and the cascading water from the sprinklers.

I looked to see if I was in the Cadillac's skid path. I wasn't, but the teen and his sandwich were. I took a quick step and just as quickly fell, the snowshoe tip digging into the ice. I unclasped the snowshoes and yelled to the teen who seemed oblivious.

The automobile caught some traction, and its aim pitched. The inside tire climbed the curb and snow plowed up over the fender. A mailbox and its post rode the hood and slid off the side taking the passenger-side mirror with it.

The automobile rode down off the curb and continued to power slide. It didn't brake as I expected but corrected and passed by the teen and me. It roared past the burning house and around with the curve and up the hill. When it disappeared from view, still going too fast, I expected to hear it crash. The airplane flew away in the sky behind me, then all was quiet.

I focused on the teen who had, sadly, consumed all but the two middle bites of the sandwich. A timber crashed inside the burning house. A second later, I heard the automobile crash.

There wasn't a skid, only the impact of rending, smashing metal. The boy was pressing the two middle bites in between his lips. He was losing the battle to contain the activity within his jacket. I looked up the curve to the sound of the car wreck.

Something inside the burning house exploded, blowing glass and wood and embers through the open doors and windows. I dropped in the snow and covered my head.

When I looked up, the outside of the large house was burning as fast as the interior, and the white lawn was littered with sinking, smoldering fragments.

The teen was using his elbows to wrestle with whatever was alive inside his jacket. His hands plied a church key on a soda can. His lunch bag was nowhere to be seen. He was turning his head side to side, extending his pink cheekbones to the warmth from across the road.

I stepped into his line of vision.

His eyes filled with alarm when he saw me.

"Hello," I offered, including a smile.

The words seemed only to upset him more. His knees clenched and locked.

The teen's brown pants were caked with snow and mud. Dried blood matted his dirty hair on the left side and stained the shoulder of his jacket.

I took a step closer.

"Are you hurt? Can I help you?"

He flinched and leaned away. I stepped back, but the alarm in his eyes remained on his dirty face. Both of us were dusted with powdery snow. I looked away.

Lights were beginning to warm the windows of the large houses along the black curve, as though synchronized, perhaps on timers. I wiped the fresh snow from my shoulders and hair. The airplane's motor was gone. The early morning was silent save the *kissing* of the lawn sprinklers.

I wanted to help him if he needed it. Clearly, he was in need. I decided to leave the teen only when I saw his fear lessen with one step away. I walked up along the road between the lit and silent houses to the automobile wreck beyond the top of the bend.

• • • •

THE AUTOMOBILE was on its side having crashed into a ditch. Its parts littered the pavement and the lawns. An old man was climbing out of the wreckage through the driver's side window. I noted the nasty tear in the nearby oak tree. He was looking at me, and when our eyes met, he raised one eyebrow, shrugged to the wreck, smiled, and waved. When he saw my flashlight, his brow furrowed.

The old man pushed snow down and away along the leaning silver roof. He climbed onto it and slid slowly down to the edge of the roadway. Standing on the pavement, he rubbed his hands together for warmth. He fingered the bruise on his cheek, which was swelling. He looked away from me and traced the path of the accident until his eyes were again on the ditch and crashed automobile. He turned at me.

"You had breakfast yet?"

I wiped snowflakes from my goggles and answered, "No."

A large sign hung from the oak he had clobbered. In green letters on a white background, it read, "Welcome to Greenland."

The old man rubbed his thin beard and his stomach and walked away.

"C'mon, then," he said. "I'm buying."

I caught up, and he pointed to my flashlight. "Good idea you put that away."

I thumbed the flashlight off, pushed it inside my jacket pocket, and followed.

We walked down the road away from the hilltop sign. Off to our right, there was a clubhouse—a two-story building of tinted windows beside an empty swimming pool and a snow-covered tennis court. I followed him across an empty parking lot past the clubhouse. He didn't say a word as he led the way across the lot to a lower street. Two minutes later, he turned to a two-story house that looked just like all the others.

I followed him to the front door, and we entered. The air inside was warm, and the front room had a cathedral ceiling and sky-blue carpet. Along the north wall was a solid row of televisions. Across the opposite wall was a line of identical cream recliners.

He led the way along a wide hall, passing a soft-lit dining room behind French doors. We entered swinging doors into a spacious white and chrome kitchen.

"Excuse me for a minute," he said.

"Sure. And thank you," I said to his back as he picked up the telephone receiver that lay on a table, its cord reaching across to the cradle on the wall.

I stepped back through the swinging doors and continued down the hall. At the end, there was an immense room at least three times the size of the television and recliner room. There wasn't any furniture. Looking up, I realized that the two-story home had no second story. The southern wall was lined with twenty-foot windows offering a view of the valley. Just outside, a white-haired woman sat at a table beneath a large umbrella. Her head and shoulders were haloed with electric blue light from a television in a weather box. Snow was falling around her and quickly melting. The heated decking under her feet was slick with water and steam rose from the boards. I returned to the kitchen.

The old man was speaking soft and low into the telephone. The warmth of the house was working on my mind and body, and even though I was hungry, I thought of lying down and dissolving into sleep.

"I'll find her first if I can," I promised.

"What was that?" the old man asked.

Before I could reply, he went on.

"Baked beans and black rye okay?"

I stretched my eyes open wide and blinked into my 3D world. I turned to him and nodded and smiled.

"Good. Maybe some coffee, too? C'mon, there's a fresh pot."

There were a dozen electric coffee percolators in a row on the tiles beside the sink. The machine nearest the tap was spitting and filling with dark brown coffee and that rich, familiar smell. The old man opened a cardboard carton on the counter next to the stove. He removed a can of baked beans and from another box lifted a similar size can of black rye bread. I had never seen bread from a can before, and I looked on as he poured dark syrupy beans into a pot on the range and put heat to it.

He pointed to the cupboard above the coffee makers. "Get us down two cups, two bowls, and two plates."

I was doing so when I heard a young woman's voice.

With my hands upward, I looked over my shoulder to her voice, sounding grainy from the receiver on the table. She spoke in low tones. Her speech was adamant, and she was pleading.

The old man asked, "Butter for your bread?"

Struggling to make out her words, I answered, "No, thank you."

The telephone went silent.

I watched the telephone and waited a minute before I joined the old man at the table with the cups, plates, and bowls. I set them out, and he nodded approval as I sat down. He moved to the range and stirred the baked beans which were bubbling and offering a sweet, warm scent. Listening for the voice from the telephone, I watched him pour coffee for himself and me.

"Thank you," I said.

He nodded twice, grinned, and went back to the stove. I took two greedy, scalding drinks from my cup.

"Mind garlic in your beans?"

Before I could answer, he set a plate of brown bread before me.

I pushed a round of black rye into my mouth and spoke through the bread.

"No, sir."

I fed myself, consuming four slices of the moist and slightly sweet bread with continuous and fast chewing.

The old man opened the cabinet door to the right of the stove and removed one of at least forty garlic powder bottles. I ate more bread while he sprinkled garlic onto the beans. He opened a drawer beside the sink and took out two spoons and a baby food jar topped with a piece of cloth. He wiped the spoons with the cloth and looking at me, said, "Sterling."

I smiled and selected another slice of bread.

He placed the pot on the table and handed me a spoon. I watched him ladle beans into my bowl.

"I don't suppose you're here to tour my fine, country living homes?" he asked.

"No. Sir. I'm..."

"Too bad. We have the finest in scenic and active living. Beautiful residences. Each with plentiful decking and expansive, private views. We offer tennis, swimming, and community activities. In addition, we offer creative and highly competitive financing."

I found myself nodding in rhythmic appreciation of this information. He refilled my bowl and raised his eyebrows in exclamation.

"A young man as yourself, perhaps married soon, starting a family, not wanting to confine his wife and children to apartment life or urban squalor, might do well to consider the type of life we offer. The type of life Greenland, California, has to offer."

He was ignoring his food and drinking his cup of coffee. I took three big spoonfuls.

"You might want to take a look around. Look at the units. There're literature and cost and financial packages in the community center lobby."

"Yes. I will," I said with my mouth full.

The old man smiled over the rim of his coffee cup. I took a large bite of round rye bread. I was taking a second bite, without having swallowed the first, when her voice rose from the telephone.

"Is that Luscious?" I said, my voice feeling slippery.

I turned to listen closer, and, because I did, it was the side of my head that struck the edge of the table.

"Christ in the clutter," were the last words I heard him say.

• • • •

I WAS climbing a leaning floor, and a baby was screaming. I watched myself climb to the window and out into a fierce wind. I grabbed tightly to the base of the radio tower atop the building, and Luscious climbed out with me. We stood in the great wind watching the beach of rusted steel plates far below. An airplane passed with faces pressed to the round windows. Most of the passengers looked horrified, but a few were drop-jawed in admiration of my bravery. I could feel Luscious right there beside me, and she was no longer scared. The building continued to tilt, and when the radio tower was parallel to the beach, I reached for her hand. I missed. I fell through the sky as the baby's cries grew louder.

I landed with my body tangled in white sheets. When my head struck the mattress, I opened my eyes to an unfamiliar dark room. I had a nauseating headache that was pushing bile into my mouth.

I could see right away that I was in a hotel room.

I turned to the nightstand and saw an empty water glass. A baby was crying, and it hurt my head and eyes. I wanted a drink of water, right away. I bottom-slid to the foot of the bed. The crying was coming from behind the door on the opposite wall.

When I stood, I vomited on the carpet. Straightening up and keeping myself perfectly still, I saw my clothes and satchel on the desk beside the dresser and mirror.

The pain that was swimming my vision left no room for thought, only observation. I slowly crossed to the door which opened to the bathroom full of painful, white light. The panicked cries were coming from the bathtub.

I pulled back the plastic curtain and looked down at the naked baby, maybe a year old, laying on a great many towels. There were five baby bottles about the infant, most of which were empty. He had messed many times, and his red face was clenched and angry as he took gasps of breath to gather volume.

I had to stop the crying. I offered a wave, to no effect.

"Please be quiet," I asked him.

The sound of my distant, thick voice peeled back a layer of the headache, and I experienced a dull inkling of curiosity.

"What's going on?"

I glanced back into the bedroom, and as he continued to cry, I left the bathroom. I watched myself put on my clothes. I pulled on my socks and boots and returned to the bathroom, and, this time, with my clothes on, I felt a bit more aware.

I noticed the tin of Similac and the tiny jars of food. I drank four handfuls of water from the tap before reading the tin and jar labels out loud over the protests from the bathtub.

I picked up one of the empty bottles from the towel-lined, badly smelling bathtub and rinsed it out. I made up a bottle of warm water just as the directions instructed. When I handed it to him and nudged his lips with the nipple, the crying stopped.

The new silence pulled another layer of pain from the headache. I ran warm water in the sink to bathe before getting a better idea. I picked up the messy baby and lay him on the bed surrounded by pillows. I ran the shower on the towels and bottles until the smears of mess were gone. The towels and bottles went into the sink. I removed my goggles and took a shower with my eyes closed.

Back in the bedroom, I began to dress again but stopped while watching the little guy. His eyes found mine, and he stared. I knelt on the bed and offered him a smile. He appeared to like that. I shivered and located the thermostat and cranked it. Back on the bed, I gave a little pull at the bottle. He yelped, so I released it.

In the bathroom, I closed the drain trap and started the shower. I went and found two blankets in the closet. With the blankets on the sink counter and the water a few inches deep in the tub, I went to get him.

It was immediately clear that he didn't like the showering water, so I changed the flow to the spout. I sat down in the water with him between my legs.

I washed his back and chest, legs and arms before wrapping him in the two blankets and patting his skin and hair dry. After nestling him with pillows on the bed, I dressed again and made up two bottles with the Similac. Placing the blankets inside the bathtub, I set the bottles on the blanket. He was falling asleep as I lay him down in the tub.

He began to cry while I put on my shoes and shouldered my satchel. The crying became more intense, and I turned but didn't stop. I opened the front door quietly and stepped outside.

Rain was falling, and I could still hear him. Rubbing the side of my aching head, I closed the door and stepped off the covered porch. I crossed the barren parking lot. While I walked the shoulder of the road, a logging truck rushed past, sending up a low filthy spray.

• • • •

MY MIND made great strides at clearing with a high intake of sugar. I chewed Ding-Dongs and Ho-Hos and Sno-Balls while rolling a cart along the four aisles of the small market. I kept the cellophane wrappers to pay for the cakes when I was done.

"You failed, you failed," was repeating in my head like a skipping record.

I had gotten no closer to saving Luscious than hearing her voice on that kitchen phone.

The words became a chant in my brain.

"You failed, you failed, you failed..."

It was a pounding accusation.

I had to stop it.

"I'll find another way!" I yelled back.

"What was that?" was called from the front of the store.

I struggled with what to do next. Notify the police? Tell them about Luscious and her captivity? Turn in the old man as well? Each thought was like a spike through the residue of the drug in my blood and mind.

I rolled the shopping cart slowly up the aisle. It was half full when I added a cowboy hat, some Vienna sausages, six cans of cola, and a map from the front of the store.

The woman at the cash register pulled my stuff along the counter and rang it up. She glanced at me one time, took in my goggles, and asked, "What's your name, kid?"

"BB Danser," I replied.

"Oh. Got yourself a stutter?"

I had no idea what she was talking about and didn't reply.

"Interesting sunglasses."

"Corrective lenses."

I paid her and stood just inside the door looking out at the rain and wondering how I was going to carry the three brown bags.

• • • •

THE BABY lay in the blankets, no longer crying, breathing in short breaths. He had a corner of a washcloth in his hands. He made a few sounds. Some were serious and some sounded like laughter. Later, he slept to the lullaby of the falling rain and the wet sweeping sound of big tires.

"What do I do with you?" I whispered to the bathroom.

No reply.

"What do I do now?"

The sleeping infant was no help. I got up from the bed and went to him.

He awoke, whelping before opening his eyes. His cry was weak, just little pulls of air surrounded by whimpers. His feet pedaled a few times. His hands reached out. He began to cry in earnest but stopped when I lifted him from the tub.

We lay side by side on the bed with my back against the headboard and the cowboy hat lowered, so it rode just over the goggles. Also on the bed were candy wrappers and infant outfits, an open box of diapers, and empty sausage tins. The room was nice and warm, and the rain provided perfect insulation. The satchel was at my side, and I had the letters from Luscious in my lap.

I reread the graphic promises and pleas for rescue. I studied the map. I went through her three letters slowly, thinking about a second attempt at rescue. My head swam with 3D images of the last twenty-four or so hours. I decided a nap might help with the headache and kill the memories. The baby's deep slumber was attractive, and I wanted some of the same.

Leaning back, I tilted the brim of the cowboy hat and covered the goggles completely.

I tried for sleep, but it alluded me.

Reaching to turn off the lamp, I saw a green envelope on the night-stand. I hadn't noticed it before.

I sat up and pulled the envelope over. My name was scrawled across the front in bold handwriting I didn't recognize.

I opened the envelope slowly.

There were two bus tickets and a letter. I unfolded the sheet of Luscious's stationery. The message was not in her handwriting.

Mister BB Danser,

You failed.

You and the other boys and girls were scammed.

Your "Luscious" is a thirty-six-year-old woman with severe mental problems, to say the least. I stopped you. I've stopped most of the others. Enclosed are two bus tickets. I'm not sure if the infant needs one or not. I found your address in your bag, and the fare will get you close to your home.

If you have thoughts of attempting another rescue, stop them.

This is your opportunity to perform a real rescue. Rescue the baby. Rescue him from his mother, that rampaging nightmare of a woman who has harmed—and worse—more than a few of your fellow comic readers.

Save the child.

Be a hero.

I'll deal with "Luscious."

It wasn't signed.

• • • •

MY PLANS to rescue Luscious were destroyed. And I had been *duped* as they say in *True Detective*.

"A *thirty-six*-year-old woman?" the words were sour bile in my throat.

"Not only tricked but also a failure," I told the sleeping baby.

I folded up the letter from the old man and slid it and her three letters inside my satchel.

Looking at the tiny boy, a new recording began to play in my head.

"Be a hero, be a hero…"

A new idea began to form, melting away some of the icy pain of the disastrous end to my long-dreamed saving of Luscious.

"I'm going to rescue you," I told the helpless baby.

• • • •

THE BABY supplies and clothing all fit into a single pillowcase. I placed a twenty on the nightstand to cover for the mess in the sink and the vomit on the carpet and the pillowcase and blanket I was taking. I decided not to ask about payment for the room because, as best I knew, I hadn't rented it.

I fed the baby some jar food of yams and mixed green vegetables. After I cleaned and diapered him, we played until he whelped for a bottle. While he sucked himself to a calm, I bundled him in a blanket, shouldered my satchel, picked up the pillowcase, and left the room.

Looking out into the rain at a passing car, I adjusted my hold on the baby and the pillowcase. I started off to my right toward the lights of town.

A few doors down the wooden walkway, a beautiful young girl about my age was holding an open, clear plastic umbrella. Her eyes were puffy and aimed across the two-lane road to the field and hills beyond. She wore a flowery dress under a bulky, blue coat.

She was speaking or chewing. I couldn't tell, but either way, she was making no sense. She wore gray wool socks and old boots. Her hand extended out into the rain where it trembled. She didn't seem to notice my footsteps. She was grinning at the water on her skin. A trail of drool fell from the corner of her lips. She appeared to be heavily drugged.

I walked closer, looking at her lovely, unblinking gaze.

She turned to me. I stopped, and she extended her rain-moistened hand.

"Where am I?" her voice was slurred.

"Near Greenland," I answered.

It appeared to mean nothing to her.

She turned her striking eyes to me and seemed duly pleased with what she saw.

"Can you help me?" she asked. "I've made a terrible mistake."

I adjusted my hold on the baby boy. Her fingertips rose and brushed my brow. Her touch was gentle, and I felt my heart fill with wonder.

"Yes," I answered. "An escape."

Her damp fingers brushed down my temple to my cheek. I saw her first smile, a small twist of relief, loopy from the drugs.

She tilted her umbrella over and above my head. She leaned and pressed her head on my shoulder. I breathed from her hair, a faint flowery scent.

Looking down, I saw the edge of a green envelope in the pocket of her big coat. We had both chased a fool's dream. Her hand glided to me, and she took my arm.

After a while, as the bus rolled along, I let her hold the baby.

ACT FOUR
INGLEWOOD

Pierce
*To enter; to penetrate; to make a way into or through something, as
a pointed instrument does; — used literally and figuratively.*

<u>Scene 8</u>

The three of us got off the bus in Inglewood, California, and I went in search of somewhere for us to stay. I found a one bedroom, third-story furnished apartment five blocks into the rundown edge of town. I paid two weeks in advance.

With the last of the drugs out of her system, I realized the girl had quite a mouth on her. Now that she was safe, she also had a mental list of expectations. Seeing the apartment for the first time, she handed me the baby and viewed the little front room with a cutting eye.

"God strike you stupid? This the best you could do?"

She scowled at the worn furniture and the peeling wallpaper and claimed the bedroom as her own.

"It's just for a while," I tried, feeling the sting.

She saw it and stepped close. A hint of a playful smile blinked to me. Her hand cupped my testicles and lifted gently, and my thoughts and hurt dissolved. She turned away and went to the bedroom.

Sitting on the couch with the baby and a jar and spoon, I called to her, "What's your name?"

"You'll call me Mother," carried from the short hall. "And while we're on the subject of names, the baby is now Pierce."

The baby and I slept that first night on the ratty couch with him on the inside curve of my body. She came of out her bedroom for breakfast. I told her a little about my former life, which didn't interest her until she heard "movies" and "Hollywood."

"You still know some of those people?" she asked, her eyes brightening as the wheels turned in her head.

Finishing her toast and juice, she left the little table. From behind her bedroom door, she called out, "Go get yourself a *movie* job."

It was a ten-mile walk each way between Inglewood and the studios, and I made those trips daily, sometimes using my thumb to save some time. On the sixth day, I got a ride on a truck with a carpenter and his Mexican crew, and the next day I started as the gopher and apprentice for this crew constructing exterior sets and props at America's Pictures.

The carpenter, Johnny John, introduced me to his crew in Spanish explaining my goggles as *lentes correctivos*. Not that they were interested. That first day was long and hard, and we were stopped three times and moved to different sets. At first, I was dangerous with a hammer, and my lower back felt bent and twisted.

After I walked home that first day, I was greeted with, "What movie stars did you see?"

"All I saw were extras standing around in a tent."

She scowled at me, an expression I had learned to accept during our first week since leaving Greenland.

I looked around our little apartment. I smelled the baby's— Pierce's—dirty diaper.

"Going to go get us dinner?" she called from behind a door.

"Yes, in a bit." I carried Pierce to the bathroom, planning on bathing both of us before going down to the deli.

The bathroom door was both closed and locked. I knocked on the door.

"Scram. I need to bathe," Mother called.

Pierce and I sat in our dirty clothes by the only window in the front room. It looked down on the slow traffic and tired, moving people in the evening light and heat.

When Mother came out into the front room, she wore new shoes and a new dress, and I saw her wearing makeup for the first time.

"What are you looking at?" she said.

I was, if anything, hungrier and even more tired. All I could think to say was, "You look nice. Bought yourself some new clothes?"

"Nope. You bought me new clothes."

That explained the thinning packet of cash in the satchel.

"Clean him up and get some sleep. I'll eat at a restaurant." With that, she left.

"You and me, *Pierce*." I tasted his name and liked its edge.

And so began our daily pattern. I would come home, and she would be gone. I learned to knock on our neighbors' doors in search of Pierce and whoever she had left him with.

On my first day off, I carried Pierce down the street to a phone booth inside a drug store. I called Mumm's message service and was told it had been canceled. I tried Ezra's number, but it had been disconnected. Holding Pierce across my chest, we walked the three blocks to a newsstand I had spotted the day before. There was nothing on Mumm in *Variety* or the *Los Angeles Times*.

"I'm not giving up," I told baby Pierce. "Just don't yet know how to find her."

• • • •

OVER THE next month, I advanced slowly up the ranks of responsibilities in Johnny John's crew, not by skill as much as attrition among the Mexicans. I saw Mother rarely. More often, I looked at her bedroom door never knowing if she was behind it or if she was out, unless she called for a meal.

I learned that America's Pictures was a B-picture studio which explained why I never saw a famous face. It was of no matter as Mother was no longer asking. The packet of cash continued to dwindle even as I replenished it with my pay.

On a Thursday six weeks after our arrival in Inglewood, I was carrying two bags of groceries to our building when I saw Mother out in *daylight*. It was the first time I had seen her outside during the day. She looked to be waiting for a ride because she stood curbside, but she was also berating one of the neighbor women who held Pierce. Mother looked pale save her red lipstick and was commanding the conversation with three of the neighbors, women she raised her nose at when around, except when they would do chores for her.

"He'll pay you." She spotted me.

I walked closer along the sidewalk as a taxicab pulled to the curb, and Mother climbed in and drove away. I joined the three women and climbed the stairs with the swirl of their foreign voices. I got the gist of their conversation—a blend of admiration for Pierce and hostility for the *bella mulher.* I relieved them of Pierce on the third-floor landing. He and I bathed, and then I made my dinner and opened baby food jars.

Ten days later, I returned home to three new suitcases sitting just inside the door and the news that we were moving. I asked, "Where to?" and received one of Mother's rare smiles—her pleased smile.

"Hollywood."

I took Pierce from the neighbor holding him when heavy footsteps came up along the landing. A big guy—one of the husbands from our floor—gathered up two of the suitcases and departed. Mother waited in her bedroom. The husband returned for the remaining suitcase which was the largest. I saw the three paper bags holding Pierce's and my belongings.

"Get your things." Mother appeared with her arms out to me. She took Pierce and handed him to a woman waiting out in the hall. I gathered up the bags, and we followed Mother down to the street.

In those days, there were many flavors of living in Hollywood. Under the royal blue skies, there were mansions and even a few castles, all under palm trees with manicured and sculptured yards and gardens and pools that no one swam in. In the backdrop, in the shadows of all the luster, there were the small enclaves where working people lived within a bus ride distance to the wealth. Our first Hollywood home was an L-shaped converted garage set back along a service alley, past the dumpsters, beside the bicycle rack for the employees of *Chef David*.

Mother hired workers and painters—no matter that I had these same skills. Hiring help was important to her. The alley house was painted an avocado green as was the front room, which she had furnished in pink, ornate elegance. The shorter part of the L was where the two small bedrooms were just past the kitchen and bathroom. Mother was pleased and, for a while, proud of our Hollywood postal code.

Our lives continued much as before—Mother worked at night at what she called "studio services," taking taxicabs. I became Johnny John's second, leaving Pierce each morning in the care of Esmeralda, our alley neighbor. In addition to caring for Pierce, she also kept the house immaculate except for Mother's green bedroom. That door was always locked.

The times that I saw Mother, which were seldom, I adored her distant beauty and graceful, studied movements and her ability to charm people to do her bidding. She would depart each night, dressed fashionably, leaving a flavor of perfume in her wake. From their porches, our neighbors would watch on as she slid into a waiting taxi, their expressions a mix of disapproval and sadness.

She continued working magic on me as well. There were occasions when we would talk briefly, in passing.

"See any stars today?" This was her frequent question.

I mentioned a couple of names, none of which were familiar to her.

"Tell your Johnny John to hitch up with an A studio," she whispered, leaning close. Her tender hand cupped and lifted my crotch.

I froze and stared.

In 3D, I adored her beautiful face and her sensual and busty figure. And her smart, alert, and lovely eyes. Within the goggles, she was the only young woman I ever saw who could alight the *boundaries* of the three dimensions and reach inside me. She melted my heart. Filled me with lust. Made a mess of my wits.

When her hand lowered to my groin, I was frozen in place, my breathing taxed.

"We need to find some private time," she would promise. Always promise.

"If Johnny John can't get you an A-studio job, find someone who will." Then she left for the night.

I recalled Mumm's similar effect on my heart and mind. While I never regretted the gift of the goggles from Ezra, I wished at times that I had received them earlier on and worn them, just once, in Mumm's presence.

• • • •

EVERY TEN days or so I would get a day off, and Pierce and I would go on bus rides. Most often to the coast. Pierce liked to stand on the window seat and watch the passing people and streets all the way from our east Hollywood home to the Santa Monica Pier. He delighted in throwing handfuls of popcorn up into the air where seagulls floated.

After his first gaze through a coin-op telescope, he filled with laughter and bobbed with delight. I learned to bring along lots of nickels on future trips to the shore. The fishermen on the pier informally adopted him as he panned the telescope and laughed, taking in the large and small boats heading out to sea.

• • • •

A YEAR passed and then a second.

Little changed. Pierce, of course, grew in size and curiosity. I stayed on with Johnny John, and Mother kept to her nighttime employment.

By the end of that second year, I had paid cash for a questionable but notarized birth certificate that introduced Pierce A. Danser to the world of the registered. It was decided that he was three years old, and that seemed about right to me.

One winter morning just after sunrise, Pierce was still asleep in his and my bed when Mother came home from the night.

"When we get married, I'm not taking your name," she told me. "I don't want to be a Danser. Your family, including your Mumm, is a bunch of nutcakes."

I stood there in my work clothes, boots in hand.

"Pierce is fortunate. He doesn't have your blood. Just your name."

She offered her right cheek, and I kissed it.

"Get to work and don't be late." She carried her purse off to her room.

That night, she went out with friends and was gone for five days.

• • • •

ON MY next day off, I left Pierce in Esmeralda's care and took the bus to within seven blocks of Mumm's mansion.

Standing at the locked, wrought-iron gates, I looked up the driveway past the manicured lawn and hedges to what little could be seen of the home I had once lived in. The day was hot, and sweat dampened my dirty work clothes. After twenty minutes, I was approached by the gardener who brushed his hands at me.

"*Vamos o llamare a la policia,*" he said, warning me off.

"Mumm?" I tried.

His eyes burrowed into me, no change, no recognition.

"Elizabeth Stark, the actress?" I tired.

"*Voy a llamar a la policia,.*" His voice cut the air.

He turned away, hedge cutters in his hand.

"*Policia* was clear to me."

• • • •

I RETURNED a week later. The gardener appeared, this time with a limb saw.

"*Vete, vago*," he growled, raising the saw.

I didn't know what the words were, but the tone was clear and familiar.

"I'll leave if you'll tell me who lives here," I said, hoping he might understand.

He surprised me by answering in English.

"This is the Harris residence. Do not come back."

After the bus ride home, Pierce and I spent the evening on the front steps of the avocado green house. Esmeralda brought out a pitcher of ice water, and while Pierce played with my goggles, I watched the staff of *Chef David* go in and out the service door.

Esmeralda joined us, taking the lowest step. She rested her wide frame and turned her beagle's face and very round eyes to me. I saw a kind sadness.

"*Tú y Pierce son escaparates*," she said.

I had heard these words before. Later, I learned that *escaparates* could be used for *window dressing*.

"You and Pierce deserve..." She stopped, struggling for the right word in English.

Esmeralda was trying again to entice me, I think, into criticism of my wife and her ways. Like other times, I refused to be drawn into her views on my little family.

Her hand reached for mine. She offered those sad, round eyes and a tender smile.

I took to avoiding her whenever Pierce wasn't at my side.

• • • •

IN THE fall of our second year in Hollywood, Mother purchased a bungalow on Vermont Avenue.

"We're now within sniffing distance of the movers in the business," she said, sharing a rare delight—a half smile and sparkling eyes.

I attended the meeting at the title company where Mother paid cash for the new home. For her own unspoken reasons, she had the documents drawn up so that the house was in my name only. I didn't understand and feared asking, not wanting to provoke her.

I packed up Pierce's and my belongings. Except for Mother's clothing trunks, everything else inside the green house was left behind. Including Esmeralda.

On my next day off, I took a bus to Mumm's mansion. The day was cold and rainy.

I had rescued Pierce. I had also rescued Mother. But Mumm's safety was a repeated haunting. I had no more clues to follow. She had vanished from all newspapers and the movie business trades. I had to know. I had to do whatever I could to see that she was safe, find out if she was alive, take her hand, and...well, I couldn't see beyond that.

I stood at the gate looking up at the mansion where she and I had once lived, now owned by a Mr. Harris, according to the gardener.

A long, black town car came down the driveway. I stepped aside as the gates opened electronically and the car rolled through. I turned to watch it leave. It came to a stop, and the rear window lowered.

"I've heard about you," a deep voice said from inside.

I walked over and looked in through the open window. I recognized Mr. David Harris, Mumm and IM's butler from years ago.

His eyes were steady on me, one brow arched.

"Please remove those," he asked, gesturing to my goggles.

I did so, rushing the normal view of the world into my brain as Mr. David Harris's eyes dissolved into smooth, dark skin. I saw a frown widen under his round nose.

"BB?" he asked.

I nodded. That was all I could do as my vision tried to orientate.

"I would invite you inside my car, but I don't want to. You're both wet and dirty. Why are you here?"

I answered with the single word, "Mumm."

"Oh, yes. Your pet name for Elizabeth Stark."

"Is she home?"

"Could be. She no longer lives here, so God only knows."

I looked up through the rain to the large home showing above the trimmed hedges. I could see lights in the second-story windows.

"This is your last visit to my home. No more," he said.

"Your home?"

Mr. Harris laughed, a deep gurgling. "Imagine that. The butler winning in the end. Might make a good movie."

"Do you know where she is?" I asked.

"You answer me this, first. Where's IM?"

I raised my goggles from around my neck and put them on.

"He's near Ann Arbor."

"Laying low? Good."

There was movement in the corner of my vision. The gardener was walking down the driveway with a baseball bat in both hands. When he reached the car, he stood beside me. Mr. Harris's hand reached out into the rain and waved him back.

"Some say your Mumm returned to England. Some say she's scattered to the four winds."

"So, she's not here?"

"You're repeating yourself. This conversation is over."

The gardener took ahold of my coat and turned me to the street as the car window went up. I was walked a couple of steps and then shoved. I watched the long, black car back up the driveway as the gates closed. The gardener stayed in position until I turned and walked away.

• • • •

JOHNNY JOHN was concerned. Our work schedules were becoming sporadic. His concern changed to alarm on a Friday when the last check from America's Pictures didn't clear.

The following Sunday, we built and furnished another two-piece set—a seedy office adjoining the main room of a luxurious home. The conversation between Johnny John and our crew was about the rumored bankruptcy of the studio.

"We'll finish this job, but if the next check bounces, we're done," he told us.

"Explain *done*, compadre?" one of the framers asked.

"Done? As in you return to the fruit fields, and BB and I find another kind of work...maybe that crap house subdivision going up in east Inglewood."

I didn't say anything, just continued standing where I had been nailing joists, but I was worried. Christmas was coming, and my cash packet was thin. You could tell by the furniture and art in our bungalow that Mother was flush with cash, but I was left carrying all the household expenses, including Mother's maid, the landscaper, and her personal shopper bills, as well as the utilities and groceries and toys and clothing for Pierce.

That Wednesday, a group of men in business suits entered Soundstage Six. Johnny John told us they were there to look over the assets as part of a purchase. I watched the men from the lighting ironwork. They didn't seem at all impressed by being in the center of the magical movie machine. I continued working as they followed the loudest talking man in through the office set and inside the adjoining front room set. They were nodding, and two men were trailing and writing on clipboards.

I recognized the loud man. It was Mr. Nash of the Mumm days, the wearer of many filmmaking hats as he wove up the studio ranks. I climbed down through the scaffolding and walked to the back door of the front room set so I would be in their way as they exited.

Mr. Nash studied me and kept talking. I lowered my goggles to my neck, and his lips frowned to one side. The men behind him were talking of escrow and capital versus expense, and Mr. Nash nodded to their voices and continued to look me over.

"Can I talk to you?" I asked.

He looked at the set door, and I opened it and stepped aside. He moved back into the luxurious front room, making way for his associates. They departed. Mr. Nash stayed back.

"I'm closing the studio down until the purchase is complete," he told me. "You want work?"

"I want to ask about Mumm."

"Who? Oh. Don't know anything about all that."

"Do you know where she is?"

"No, I don't. Your father is insane—that's a given. All I know is that something happened, and he was almost certainly behind her disappearance."

One of the businessmen called to Mr. Nash from the edge of the set. I watched him take out a gold box and carefully select one of many business cards.

"I often need deliveries made. You interested in being a delivery boy? If so, call that number."

With that, he stepped down from the set and joined his associates on the soundstage floor. I watched them leave through the main door, stepping out into a brilliantly lit winter day. I put my goggles back on and returned to work.

• • • •

WHEN THE next check bounced, Johnny John took us all out to breakfast and paid each of us what he could, about half of what we were owed, from his own wallet.

That evening, I called the number on Mr. Nash's card. He didn't answer. A bored but sugary female assistant took my call.

"Where do you live?" she asked.

"On Vermont in Hollywood."

"Do you own an automobile?"

"No."

"Have a garage?"

"Yes. Do you want my name?" I asked.

"Don't need that. You dialed this number. Is it a carport or a garage with a door? Is it cluttered or does it have room for a vehicle?"

I thought of the detached garage at the bungalow with nothing but saw horses and yard tools in it. "It's a garage. I need to clean it out, but—"

"Does it have a good door?"

"Yes, well, sure."

"Can it be locked?"

"I'm sure it could be, yes. Can I speak to Mr. Nash?"

"No, you can't. Can you start now? If not, I've got other applicants."

"I can start today if needed."

"Okay, give me your number. A man will call you at eleven. He'll bring you up to speed."

I wanted to ask again to be switched to Mr. Nash, but the call clicked off.

• • • •

THE BIG advantage to my new job was that I could use the loaned auto for my personal needs, as long as I obeyed Rule Number One and took the car home every night and locked it up in the garage. I was paid in cash by the same man who delivered the car. We met for the first time at a donut shop a few blocks from the closed down America's Pictures. The money was very good—twice what I had made working for Johnny John.

Pierce had a delightful Christmas. He and I and Mother's maid were sitting on the floor before the ornate and elegant Christmas tree Mother bought and had delivered. There were toys and coloring books and new clothes. With the cash packet once again expanding, he and I resumed our *idyllics* to the Santa Monica Pier and the telescope Pierce was fascinated with.

Rule Number Two of the delivery business was to keep the interior of the old Chevrolet immaculate. I bought a used vacuum for the garage and ran it daily. I also cleaned the back seats and kept what I found in the creases of the seats. I started a collection using a coffee can at first until there was so much stuff that I switched to a grocery carton—lipsticks and coins and underwear and little bottles of different shapes and size.

Rule Number Three was never to wash the exterior of the Chevrolet, except the windshield. After a time, the automobile's original color was indistinct under layers of grime and dust. The man at the donut shop told me to get a second, private telephone installed at the house which I did. He increased the cash payments to cover the expense.

• • • •

WHEN THE movie studio reopened, it was called Dashing Nash Movies. The next time the donut-shop man and I met, he offered me a second job with the film crew. I was told to be ready to have my day's work interrupted at any time to make deliveries, and I readily agreed.

By the end of the month, I was soon adding to a second packet of cash, even as Mother's expenses increased. Things were looking up, and my new job was interesting. I was in a camera crew—the mechanical side—modifying and setting up dollies and cranes, and after another month, operating the camera rigging. Eventually, I was promoted to assisting with the cameras themselves.

Sometimes there were delivery issues. The girls I transported at night were often giddy, chatty, and nervous and had many questions I couldn't answer. At or near dawn, as I drove them home from Mr. Nash's mansion, or the equally large homes of his associates, I often had to assist them because they were heavily medicated. Sometimes they got sick along the way, both to and from. There were also times when I would deliver two girls, but only one required a ride home.

I delighted in learning the cameras. After two months, I was occasionally asked for my ideas on lens selection and framing which I seemed to have a knack for. Four months in, I was assigned the formal title of second assistant cameraman to a low-budget and quickly filmed title. I was responsible for the set-up and maintenance of the cameras as well as logging in and securing the film reels.

A week after Pierce's fourth birthday party, we made another move. This time to a two-story Hollywood residence with large yards and a swimming pool and cabana. Mother had the place painted and furnished before we moved in. Like before, the house was placed in my name. I was curious but didn't ask.

The house was what in those days was called an entertainment home with the entire first floor designed for dress-up parties. Mother had the second story to herself, which had a parlor front room, an office with telephones and nice desks for her assistants, and beyond, the locked door to her vibrant green bedroom. The detached, two-car garage was set to the back of the property past the swimming pool and cabana. Pierce and I were delighted to move into and enjoy one of the two guest cottages with a private lawn right at the water's edge.

Pierce and I didn't see much of Mother. We could rarely tell if she was home or off on her three to five-day trips. She would call the guesthouse from the main house if she needed to see either of us.

Pierce took to water well and was soon water safe and adventurous. He built wooden boats in the garage which he liked to launch and swim alongside. As long as we didn't make much noise, we enjoyed the pool all year round.

In the fall of that year, there was some sort of labor dispute at the studio. The nameless donut-shop man directed me to ignore the pickets, and I received a bonus as well as a promotion to first assistant cameraman on Dashing Nash Movies' next film. The film and production crews were short-staffed, and people often came or disappeared during the production.

The donut-shop man told me to improve my clothing. I called Mother from the guesthouse asking for advice. Another woman answered. That same day, her assistant came down from the big house with a shopping list. There was a personal note on the list instructing me to "continue to wear work boots as it sends a good message to the studio."

By that night, I had three solid black suits, five white oxford shirts, and three solid green ties.

The first film I was assigned to was to be shot in 3D. The working title was *Lost,* and the parts of the storyboards I was assigned to were the trolley shots through shops and alleys, crowds, a zoo, and an airport terminal. As first assistant cameraman, I was occasionally allowed to operate the cameras as well as do the focus markings and lay out routes with different colors of gaffing tape. I had little sense of the overall story but overheard the assistant director, the AD, talking with the production crew.

"This one's going to knock it out of the park."

"How so?"

"Racy and tense and all those fools paying extra for their cardboard viewers."

Ira Gersham was the film's camera operator and my boss. He was a wizard with the dual 3D camera equipment, and we worked closely together. I learned a great deal. A friendship, of sorts, developed. He had a workshop where he taught me how to maintain the cameras and where he engineered experimental equipment that we put into use, refining how the dual lenses adjusted to the quick movement. The downside for 3D audiences came from when the technology wasn't utilized properly. Nausea and headaches and eyestrain were the major complaints.

He was taken with my goggles and often tried them on. He loved a steady viewing but got queasy with a few steps. After a time, he engineered an improved pair for himself, and we walked and talked within a 3D world, except when manning the cameras during shoots.

One-third of the way through the seven-week shoot, the picketers were joined by television cameras. We started having a hard time getting to work when the union figured we were sneaking in through the back-street access. On the set, work became unfocused and erratic. We lost a third of our crew including our director of photography, the DP, the set designers, two ADs, and half of the construction crew.

Mr. Nash came to the soundstage, shut everything down with a command, and gathered us around him.

"You are now a hearty band of pirates. We drop formal titles and roles and get creative and flexible. If you are even close to being able to fulfill a function, it's your new job."

By that afternoon, the prior camera department of seven was two—Ira and me. We also worked together on set construction and prop layouts and story continuity. Things got worse with the picketers and the press, so we spent the last twenty-three days of production living at the studio. This meant that my delivery jobs were canceled. I missed Pierce and called him every evening. He was in the care of Mrs. Hilda Beck, whom Mother had hired, and I paid.

I was able to slip out of the studio one night just after sunset when the pickets thinned for dinnertime. I put the Chevrolet in the garage and found Pierce and Hilda Beck leaving the guesthouse and walking to the swimming pool. I had talked to Hilda a couple of times when I called and had not formed an opinion. She walked stiffly in front of Pierce who carried another boat cobbled together from scraps of wood, hinges, nails, and odds and ends. Her voice was firm and crisp, and Pierce was nodding and ignoring her as they passed through the gate to the pool area. She was tall and thin and wore a formal caregiver outfit complete with matching black shoes, black dress, and a doily neckline buttoned all the way to her chin.

I followed them with my eyes. From what I was seeing and hearing, I was not pleased. Or at least not until they were at the water's edge where Pierce climbed the steps down into the pool and gently cast the boat out. Hilda surprised me by removing her shoes and sitting down on the pool-side placing her long stockinged legs in the water. I watched Pierce reach back for her hand, and she took it, and the two of them smiled warmly to one another. They looked excited and pleased with the sturdiness of the boat, and both were chatting and pointing.

I remained at the gate, and while I wanted to join in on the fun, I stayed put. I watched Hilda look once to the big house before she slid into the pool and waded to Pierce's side, still in her black dress. The two of them pushed at the water and laughed as the boat took to the waves. I watched Pierce submerge and swim underwater to the little boat which he turned and nudged in her direction. She clapped her hands and laughed in delight while lowering her shoulders under the surface.

He was happy. She was happy. I went to the garage, unlocked it, and drove the Chevrolet back to the studio.

• • • •

MORE OFTEN, my storyboard ideas were taken up. The remaining bigwigs began to rely on me for story action ideas and solutions. I helped with transitions that propelled the film forward. I was good with suggestions that maintained momentum, which in Hollywood was more of a priority than plot continuity or logic.

During postproduction, titles were assigned for the credits. I received my first, "screenplay by." My name was third at the bottom with Mr. Nash's at the top.

The strike ended during the last week of postproduction. By that time, our hearty band of pirates was working well together, and we were allowed to finish the film without the involvement of the returning employees.

Lost was a success, at least on the scale of the B pictures that Dashing Nash Movies made. The critics berated it, but Mr. Nash couldn't care less. The film began turning a solid profit and was popular with audiences. The daring use of fast action and 3D ran nicely against the grain of current cinematic trends. While *Lost* was referred to as a dual gimmick, Mr. Nash was often smiling and laughing when he left the studio for the bank with the weekly proceeds.

The European press had a love affair for *Lost*, seeing in it a serious and meaningful importance that was lost—pun intended—on all of us at Dashing Nash Movies.

• • • •

OUR PRESTRIKE roles and lives returned, and four days later, I was back in the nighttime delivery business. I continued paying Hilda and the rest of Mother's staff and all the household expenses and was still able to save some cash which I banded and stowed with the original packet.

At the studio, the joke was that I had pretty good story vision—never mind the goggles. The next film I was assigned to was *Runner*, a chase and escape story set in a war-torn residential neighborhood not unlike those on the far outskirts of Los Angeles. The format was to be 3D again but in Technicolor this time. Ira and I were the only two proponents of the use of 3D. Mr. Nash was won over slowly as he and his producers were wary of the additional production and distribution costs of the format.

"3D's a fad with short legs, but let's roll the dice again," Mr. Nash announced.

The delivery business was steady and profitable. I was escorting young women to and from the palatial homes of Mr. Nash's constantly newfound friends and to his place as well. I was stopped and briefly arrested four times during the next year. When this happened, the young ladies were whisked away after telephone calls and cash payments were made by Mr. Nash's studio assistants. After the fourth stop, the Chevrolet was stocked with cash in paper bags in the trunk. From then on, when I was pulled over, I was let go after an exchange at the rear of the automobile.

At the studio, *Runner* came out of preproduction with me on a trial basis as both first assistant cameraman and script supervisor. This was a fast rise through the ranks and surely a benefit of being an original member of the strike-breaking band of pirates.

During that same year, Pierce started school, escorted to and from by Hilda. He was taken with the cameras I would bring home—the smaller units that had been cast aside and were in need of repair. He, like me, was happiest when within a viewfinder. Ira came by often, and we three boys tinkered with standard and 3D movie equipment.

Eventually, a lab of sorts came together in the garage beside the guesthouse. As time allowed, we made six short movies. For locations, we used the garage, the swimming pool, and our little house. The yard and guesthouse began to look like a movie set as we added lighting and props. Pierce's biggest hit was *The Sinking of the Big Boat* filmed poolside and in the water. Hilda would often take a patio chair from the umbrella table and sit to our side. She and Ira had developed a conversational bond, perhaps a romance. In the fall of that year, the filming of *Runner* was completed, and we moved quickly into postproduction.

The rain in Los Angeles fell hard, and there was flooding on the Thursday Hilda came down from Mother's stately and prim mansion and interrupted us. Pierce and I were testing our first waterproof camera casing, and he was describing the next shot. Seeing Hilda's worried expression, I climbed out of the pool and joined her at the umbrella table.

"Your wife is in trouble. I had to talk to two detectives."

I drove downtown and paid her bond from the cash in the Chevrolet's trunk which I later replenished from my own packets. I offered Mother a ride and was waved off. Her assistant, the focused and effective Danielle, was at the ready at the police station driveway. I stood in the rain as Mother was assisted into her long, pink Lincoln. Her face was bruised and cut, and she walked as though her hips or lower back were injured. Danielle handed her a pair of dark glasses and a scarf.

After this incident, things inside Mother's mansion changed—a telephone switchboard was installed with more phones and desks added to her upstairs office. Hilda became my eyes and conduit as Mother was no longer talking to me. Hilda told me about the staffing of the telephones and Mother's living exclusively behind the double doors to her bedroom suite, except to attend the parties of mostly elderly rich women and barely dressed young men.

Following her arrest, I didn't see Mother for the rest of 1955 and for several years after that.

On a Friday, the phone in the guesthouse rang at 4:00 a.m. It was the normal—a transport was requested from Mr. Nash's residence. Pierce was asleep in his little bed when I left to make the predawn trip.

The gates to Mr. Nash's residence opened as I turned in onto the steep driveway. I drove to the back of the house to the staff entrance under an ivy-draped atrium. All was still, and the dark morning was cold. A single light bulb shined over the back steps and door.

When the door opened, two young ladies were assisted to the Chevrolet. Both of them were disheveled, their clothing askance, their makeup rubbed away, and their movements sedated. I hadn't delivered these two ladies to Mr. Nash's the evening before, but I recognized one of them as Father's one-time companion, Heidi Ho. Heidi sat beside the other who went limp in the back seat, bent over forward so that her gold hair was splashed over her knees, and her arms hung to the floorboard.

Heidi pulled on a pair of sunglasses with trembling hands. She dabbed at the corner of the swollen lips of her familiar face with a piece of cloth that was red with her own blood. I watched her aim her sunglasses at the roof of the back seat and spill against her door, making incoherent, but insistent sounds. The porch light was extinguished, and I steered the Chevrolet down into the Hollywood streets without a word. If she recognized me, she didn't say so. But I had known her pregoggles, and besides, it had been a few years.

At a well-lighted boulevard intersection, I braved, "Heidi?"

"Huh? Wha…" she replied in a pained lisp.

"Heidi. Heidi Ho. Do you remember me? IM's son. BB?"

"Just drive the car, moron." Her voice was hostile, and she kept her sunglasses aimed at the roof not lowering to my mirror.

"Right. Yes."

At the next intersection, I spoke up again. "Is there anything I can do for you? Help you?"

She laughed, her voice soggy. "Gonna rescue me?" She laughed some more.

I had their addresses written on notepaper that one of the house staff had given me.

At the first stop, a tall and thin apartment building, a man came out and carried the girl with the splashing gold hair from the car. We didn't speak.

We were pulled over four blocks down Vine Street, and at first, it looked like the normal kind of stop. The police car parked behind us, washing the rear window with hot light. I waited with my hands-on display on the steering wheel. The officer didn't approach at first. He waited until three more police cars arrived which had never happened before.

When I was told to get out of the car, I went to the trunk and offered each of the officers a paper bag of cash. A pair of aviator sunglasses shook side to side in the predawn light while the bags were handed out. The voice under the shades said to me, "This don't cut it. Your Mr. Nash has been delinquent."

I knew about the biweekly *donations* Mr. Nash made to the police, having been asked to deliver these from time to time.

"Let me call his office—" I started to say when a billy club struck my ribs hard and a fist punched the side of my head. Three sets of boots began kicking as I first knelt, then lay prone on the pavement. I was awake long enough for the initial explosions of pain, bombs going off on all parts of my body. Then everything went black.

I woke in an infirmary in the rear of a police station. I lay there with tubes and bandages, my goggles gone, the only sound coming from the medical equipment and the rain on the window high up on the wall. No one entered the room the first day, not a nurse, not a doctor. I wasn't going anywhere—my right ankle wore a thick leather strap connected to the bed frame with a chain.

The window up on the wall became a black square at night, and the only light in the room was the faint green glow of the bulbs of the medical equipment. When the door finally opened, I watched a large man enter from the light in the hall. He wore a long coat and a dark fedora. I watched him cross the foot of the bed. He scraped a chair to my side and sat down with a grunt.

"Your Mr. Nash has gone down. Hard. No more movies. No more of his sickness with girls. We don't need your testimony, which you should appreciate. We're not even gonna have you sign the statement that's been written on your behalf. A Mr. Ezra Mayer has yanked a few chains, greased your slide, if you will. And speaking of your slide, yours is at an intersection. But no worries, okay, Mr. Danser? We've made some choices for you. You've got two more days here to heal up, and then your whole new life begins. Rest up, boy."

I wanted to ask for an explanation. I wanted to ask about what happened to Heidi Ho. I asked the officer if he knew where my goggles were. He pointed to the nightstand as he left the room.

ACT FIVE
DRIFTWOOD

View
*To see; to behold; especially, to look at with attention, or for the purpose
of examining; to examine with the eye; to inspect; to explore.*

Scene 9

I was greeted warmly by the recruiter, who was expecting me and had my ASVAB results, though I'd never taken the test. Someone had completed all of my paperwork prior to my arrival including my request for a seat in the Seabee school. All I really had to do the first two days was take the oath, watch my long, black hair get buzzed to the floor, and remove my goggles.

I didn't mind the missing hair, but parting with the goggles was difficult. There was no choice, and I was told I could keep them with my few other personal belongings. Within twenty-four hours, I was functioning well without them. There was no reason for eye contact, which wasn't possible. Instead, I followed verbal orders constantly screamed into our faces.

I called the guesthouse every chance I got. Hilda reassured me that Pierce was well, and they were doing fine.

"Thank you, and give him my love."

I also told her where the cash packets were.

• • • •

MY FELLOW recruits and I were marched onto a train where we spent the next two days traveling to boot camp. It was two days and nights in a crowd of voices, most of us sleeping on the floor.

On the military base, I discovered that I made a good Seabee—a puppet, if you will—staying on course with instructions and orders without questioning, without thinking. Those weeks were a blurred scramble of fall in, fall out, before dawn to way past dark. It was a swirl of intense mental and physical training including close-order drills and long marches and classes on shipboard conduct. I learned to live in close quarters with strangers in bunks stacked three high.

Later, there was construction operations training before I was sent to an adjunct specialty school for filming documentaries and camera operations and maintenance. That was followed by three weeks of basic combat training where I was qualified on different weapons and learned how to set up defensive perimeters for combat zones.

Following the completion of combat training, I received deployment orders and took another train trip. I was assigned to administrative duty in SFAC—the Seabee Film Archive Center.

I quickly learned my new duties. I worked in film restoration and archive filing, learning the indexing system that made no sense, but was also perfectly logical, I was told. During this assignment, I discovered the massive library of stereoscope reels. During World War II, 3D images had played a big part in measuring details of terrain and structures for bombing. I enjoyed the work, and the assignment was eerily appropriate for my qualifications making me wonder if strings had been pulled and by who.

Midway through my first six months, I received my first—and only—stateside parcel. Six-year-old Pierce and Hilda had baked a dozen sugar cookies which arrived in crumbs inside the battered box. I savored each broken bit, eating them slowly over the next two weeks. In my next letter to Pierce, I wrote:

My darling Pierce,

Thank you for the wonderful cookies. I love that you helped make them.

I miss you and will be home as soon as my tour of duty ends. Please stay close to Hilda's side.

I can't wait until we are back to making movies.

You are in my heart,

Dad

• • • •

I **HAD** the archive films and the stereoscope reels to live within during the day. When off duty, I took to studying the sky from within my 3D goggles. Often the moon brushed my cheeks as the stars tapped and tickled the tip of my nose and brow.

It was during one of my rooftop *idyllics* that I was visited by Lieutenant Ezra Mayer, who climbed the ladder to where I lay on the tarpaper. He sat down beside me. I quickly sat up to salute his seniority, but he waved that off.

"At ease. Hello, BB. If you've been wondering who has been guiding your path in the service, look no further. Your training has been sculpted, you might call it."

"Yes, sir."

"Drop the formalities. For right now, we're just a couple of movie makers up on a roof."

"Sir?"

"Ezra, please. A long time ago...I was inappropriately and madly in love with your mother, your Mumm." His words sounded as though planned carefully.

In the following silence, I aimed my goggles at the moon and stars.

"Sir...Ezra, where is she?" I asked.

"She...departed."

"Is she alive?"

Ezra lay back fully and viewed the night sky.

"That's the magic of a film career," he said in a contemplative tone. "She lives on. Forever. Shame that she can't duck out from under those plodding scripts."

"Sir, what happened to her?"

"It's Ezra. And that's your mystery to unravel. Your puzzle to find the pieces to and put together. I can't help you with that. Before she left me—left us—she asked that I do what I could for you. And I have. When your duty is complete, you should be well set for a studio career. That said, I am now casting you off."

"Sir, you haven't answered any of my questions."

"That's true. I can offer you this. You're being reassigned. You'll be documenting a clandestine operation. A rescue. It's off the books. Before you ship out, buy yourself a transistor radio."

"Sir?"

"No more talk. Relax. Lay back. View the heavens, or heaven, if you prefer."

• • • •

WHEN MY orders came, I went to the base store and bought a wallet-size AM radio.

Eleven days later, I was aboard a large ship where I was introduced to the five Seabees and four Specwar soldiers we would be supporting. We were assigned tight quarters in the metal belly of the ship near the bow segregated from the Navy personnel up above. Lt. Madera led the Specwar guys, and we reported to Lt. Dirks, who was tall and soft-spoken and very smart. Our two groups tried to get along, but we spoke different languages. There was some mutual joking and laughter during meals, and that was about it.

We were at sea for twenty-three days during which I learned as much as I could from my fellow Bees. The Seabees have many specialties—airmen, fireman, seaman, and many more. Our team was made up of construction men. Lt. Dirks ordered my camera equipment to remain stowed as I listened and learned about their expertise and plans.

We debarked on a moonless night into calm seas, the nine of us and all our supplies loaded onto a motorized pontoon. We reached shore without incident and worked throughout that first night unloading and setting up a base camp under the supervision of Dirks. The Specwars got their supplies to shore and disappeared into the trees. Using the draping of the jungle for additional camouflage, we constructed their camp and ours two hundred yards up the rocky beach. Seabee Near was assigned to security as the sun rose, and we tented for three hours of sleep.

I awoke to heat and humidity and swarming, low clouds of sand flies. I sprayed my skin and face with repellent as I looked down to the shore and the sea. The transport ship was gone.

The mealtime chatter was that we were near an oil depot that wasn't on any maps. Lt. Dirks pulled all five of us together and explained that our first task was to build a bridge over a river I could hear but hadn't seen. I was ordered to film the construction and help in any way I was asked or ordered.

The talk was that the bridge was for civilian use, though no roads were connected to it. That first day, our work was started, stopped, and redone for the training film. I filmed with a 16mm handheld. These starts and stops were not my doing. Specwar Lt. Madera had different thoughts on the focus of the film. He wanted to be the star. He was a lean, tan, muscular officer in his late twenties, a handsome man whose uniform fit better than most. Now that we were on shore, he took to wearing a pair of very dark sunglasses above his fine nose. He was letting a mustache grow in. He and his men didn't work on the bridge but were featured in their armed and ready security movements and positions.

Fifty yards up into the trees and growth, the river straightened out for twenty yards, and this was where the bridge would be built. We had winches and saws, cables and jacks. Two sections of our landing pontoon were dismantled and used as the primary crossing structure. We also moved and used trees and stone. The bridge was at the head of our track from the beach and just a way from a basin that filled from a twenty-five-foot waterfall.

We worked with our shirts off, our skin smeared with sunblock and bug spray. The work was difficult and exhausting, and during our ordered breaks, rules and regulations were relaxed. Some smoked cigarettes when not gulping water. In my case, I asked for permission to wear my 3D goggles—my corrective lenses.

Madera gave my goggles a single arched eyebrow, nodded approval, and barked, "Go see that your movie cameras are at the ready."

The 16mm handheld was good to go. I unpacked two cans of fresh film to take to the next shoot. The left side of my equipment crate held the hefty, military-designed stereovision camera under its tripod and film cans. I was loading that camera with two reels of film and mounting it on the tripod when I was ordered back to bridge construction. I covered the camera with canvas to protect it from the probable rains and definite humidity.

We were ordered back to camp at sunset for a meal of MREs.

"Eat quick," I was ordered. "You have night duty."

I was told to march down to the shore and stand guard.

I stood in the sand at the tree line and watched the moonless, western sky and silver waves washing the rocks.

Late that night, when the sky was black silk and the stars were tapping my face and fingertips, I heard distant voices carrying from the jungle. They were the sounds of a party punctuated by small arms fire.

• • • •

AT FIRST light, I was relieved by Dirks, who looked like a train wreck survivor. His eyes were red, his movements had lost all confidence, his lips were wet, and he was mumbling to himself. He didn't take up the post but led me back into the jungle.

The camp looked like the scene of Dirks' train wreck. The fire was out, and men were sleeping here and there, wherever they had dropped at the end of the night.

Madera was the only man awake. He stood at the far side of the clearing, hip high in the green brush with the jungle rising high above and around him. He was sharpening a machete with a square stone, his eyes harsh on his efforts while he talked to himself in Spanish.

Without looking up, he spoke to Dirks, who ordered me to "Get some winks before 0800."

Sleep came fast in my shaded tent with the front flaps open in case we got a breeze. When I was woken two hours later by Nears just outside my tent, all the Seabees were up and about. The fire had been rebuilt and stoked, the camp was cleaned up, and there was order once again. A quick breakfast was eaten, and by 0830, we were looking and acting orderly. Madera pulled us together at the radio pack on a large, granite rock. Three of the four Specwars appeared, and Madera gave us our new orders.

"We are going to build an airstrip."

Referencing his map, he explained that the site was eleven clicks away.

"We'll be moving all equipment to the next location and setting up a new camp."

I was ordered to film the packing and the departure of the team and then gather my camera and follow.

Two hundred yards into the foliage, we started climbing a narrow footpath that rose across the face of the southern cliff. Fifty yards up, we came to the first in a series of landings cut into the rock. From there, we carried equipment up a series of Z's that traversed the mountain face. The climb was slow, but we completed it two hours before sunset when we were informed that the return trip would be used to improve the trail.

Working with pry bars, picks, shovels, and machetes, we worked downward, widening the trail and carving steps in the rock under ripe, green foliage. We also dug and moved stones to expand the mid-turn landings, which had views of the sea below. These, we were told, would later be used as sentry posts.

As ordered, I split my time between manning a shovel and pick and filming Madera's skilled and firm leadership of our efforts. After we had cut the second sentry post, I filmed him standing strong and tall with the western sky at his back pointing and giving orders.

At nightfall, I was ordered down to our first camp to guard it. The two teams climbed away up the mountain to set up the second camp.

It took all the following day to finish the work on the steep trail and carry our remaining supplies up to the new camp. As before, my machete and shovel work was stopped from time to time by Madera to film him and the construction work. Our second camp was at the edge of a field of a crop gone to seed.

Standing in the shade of the high jungle, I was opening an MRE and trying to decide what the crop in the field had been.

"Have a banana?" Dirks offered from behind.

I turned, and he held out a small bunch—a few were yellow, but most were green. I accepted the bananas and watched him cut another bunch with the sharp edge of a hoe from the tree overhead.

"Tomorrow, we're going to turn that mess into an airfield," he said as he chewed and pointed.

I looked out into the overgrown field. It was eighty yards wide and nearly a half-mile long.

"How?" I asked.

He handed me the hoe.

"Just kidding," he said, laughing.

I was again ordered to night security detail, and I was given four phosphorus flares to be placed twenty yards apart, forming a square in the north end of the field. I was told to light them at 0200.

I headed out while one of the Specwars distributed small tin cans and rags to all the men standing around the low campfire. I walked to the north end of the field with my four flares listening to their voices growing loud in a mix of laughter and confusion. I had stowed my transistor radio in my pocket thinking I might get reception from the top of the mountain.

At 0200, I lit the first flare. Ten minutes later, the four corners of a square were formed by white phosphorous. The white light from the flares was both blinding and beautifully sparkling, filling my goggles and fluttering on my cheeks and nose.

The helicopter came into view fast and loud, rising to the mountaintop from the ocean. It waddled above the phosphorus square just long enough to release an immense pallet that landed heavily, shaking the ground under my boots. The cables were released, and the helicopter flew away. We had been resupplied, including two odd-shaped vehicles.

The flares extinguished around the shapes before I could make out what they were. I assumed my fellow Bees would come out, and we would begin unloading, but I was wrong. After waiting a half hour, I sat down in the sticky, fragrant field looking up into the stars. In the distance, the team's sporadic and chaotic voices carried off and on. When automatic gunfire scattered loudly, I was glad to be lying low in the hemp grass.

• • • •

AT DAWN, I watched Near enter the field. He walked on uncertain feet and was weaving and whimpering to himself. He gave the pallet a half glance, nodded to me, and said, "You're relieved."

Without another word, he lay down on his side and pulled his knees up to his chest.

Back at the camp, I set up my tent and found sleep. An hour later, I was startled awake by the rumbling start of vehicle engines from the field.

Over the next eight days, the mountaintop was plowed under and graded. The field was leveled and then compacted. I alternated between camera work and manning hand tools as ordered. In the evening of the eighth day, Madera climbed up on the side of the bulldozer and spoke with Near, who was operating the vehicle. The two talked for a few minutes while referencing the map that Madera held.

Near drove the bulldozer to the southwestern end of the airstrip and turned into the jungle cutting a single swath, forming a rough and narrow track. I set up to film this and was ordered to stand down, so I stood and watched the bulldozer disappear into the far jungle. Both teams were ordered back to camp. From the west, I could hear the faint puffing and plowing of the bulldozer. Around sunset, it went silent. Neither he nor the bulldozer were ever seen again

The evening's campfire was rebuilt, and as the sky darkened, Madera handed out the tin bottles and small, white cloths, skipping me, as usual. He stood at the edge of the field facing us, his machine gun on his shoulder, holding his own bottle and rag. I was breaking down one of the tripods and packing the cameras and film for the night, and I paused to watch Dirks. He tipped his silver bottle into his cloth, took a deep breath from it, and collapsed beside the fire with his boots on the hot stones. I walked over and pulled his boots and legs back from the flames and picked up his bottle, which lay just beyond his prone hand. I put the cap back on.

"Camera grunt, head out," Madera ordered.

I stood and slung my rifle and read the bottle label. Ether-something—the rest of the word was medical gibberish.

The others were laughing and pointing at Dirks and his "overdoing it." I walked out onto the airstrip and took up my usual position on the hard grade close to the original location of the four flares. Sitting with my knees raised, I scanned the four ends of the airstrip. The voices from camp began their usual rise and collapse with laughter along with the chaos of their stumbling about.

In the southwestern sky, the dense, high treetops were black, and beyond there was a man-made illumination, a skyward glow, from deep within the jungle.

Like the past nights, I took out my transistor radio and thumbed the dial slowly along the pickets of wavering static. I had yet to get anything like a station, but two nights before, I thought I had heard a male voice, perhaps standing in automobile traffic, speaking Spanish. The batteries had nearly run down, but I thumbed the dial slowly, nonetheless. I aimed the extended antenna in all four directions before I settled to the north. Maybe it was the cloudless black sky that made the difference. I'll never know. The dial scrolled over a man's dry voice concluding what I thought was a newscast. As my thumb minutely adjusted the dial, his voice rose and fell within borders of static. He went silent for six seconds and was replaced by commercial music. The last note of the jingle was still ringing when a woman's voice began speaking. "...Luxurious travel aboard World-wide Airlines' fleet of commercial aircraft."

She had a British accent, and I sucked in the deepest breath of my life.

It was Mumm, I was certain. The unique, intelligent lilt and a crinkle, a glimmer, of humor and wit. The commercial ran nearly to the end before dissolving into static. I spent the rest of that night thumb brushing the dial, the antenna aimed north, hoping for another Worldwide Airlines commercial. I recall the view of the little radio through my goggles, which I studied throughout the night until day's first glow. I recall the hours of ear straining, focusing on the silence.

Dirks came for me and followed me back to camp instead of lying down as before. I was ordered to get four hours of sleep.

Madera woke me. He had pulled a cobbled chair over to the front of my tent and sat in it as I stirred and began dressing.

"Relax, Seabee. Clear the sleep from your brain."

I splashed canteen water on my head and face, rubbed them both, and pulled on my goggles, which appeared to amuse him.

"Everybody's having visions. Even you. With those."

I pulled on my boots.

"Today is going to get interesting," he said. "Tense, too. I need your cameras set up midway on the airfield on the east side. Place them in the brush, so they aren't visible to us. At 1300, begin filming the mouth of that tunnel, the one I had Near carve. You'll see me appear, and you're to follow me. Well, film me and a new compadre as we walk along the airfield to the camp. I'll signal you when to stop."

Madera gathered both teams together around the morning fire.

"When coherent..." he told both groups, "...some of you might have a question or two about what our mission is. Here is the answer...you get no answers. This effort doesn't need to make sense to you. Today we will place the last piece of the puzzle, but you still won't see clearly. Never will. Aim your addled brains away from that. We will be heading home tomorrow and back inside the United States by midweek. We are on the crest. Today we will be conducting an exchange. Any questions?" he asked rhetorically, shaking his head.

At 1100, Madera unslung his rifle, unholstered his sidearm, and pulled on a heavy backpack. He beckoned to me, and he and I walked in silence to the middle of the airstrip where I turned away to set up the cameras in the bush. He continued up the hard-packed airstrip to the bulldozed tunnel.

At 1230, I had the 3D cameras loaded and focused in a medium shot that would track with a zoom at a walking pace. The mouth of the tunnel was centered.

At 1258, I turned those cameras on and raised the handheld. The wind was sweeping dust spirals onto the airstrip—a bank of low, heavy clouds was coming in off the ocean to deliver midday rains. I kept my eye to the viewfinder, mindful of the change of fragrance in the air, from damp foliage to metallic. The scent made my ears ring.

At 1301, the rains began. Madera walked from the tunnel. He was centered in the viewfinder from his belt to the foliage around his head and sweaty face and satisfied smile. I widened the frame and saw that his backpack was gone and that he had company—a blindfolded civilian in a filthy business suit. The man had a pale, reptile face and was talking fast and following in Madera's footsteps. Madera was ignoring the man as the two walked out onto the airstrip and started for the distant camp.

When they were twenty yards out, I shut down the handheld and moved to the 3D cameras to film a slow pan of their walk. The businessman began to rant and wave his arms and was still being ignored by Madera who turned once to my cameras and winked dramatically. The rain fell heavily from the dark cloud above. I adjusted the apertures to compensate for the gray light. I filmed Madera and the man in his dirty suit all the way along the airstrip.

They were thirty strides from the camp when I heard the sound of a vehicle to my left. I continued to film and raised my eye from the viewfinder and looked to the tunnel mouth. Seeing nothing, I reentered the viewfinder and filmed the businessman going into a panic and looking back up the airstrip. I considered a cut and pan to the tunnel but chose to do as ordered and kept the focus on the two men.

When Madera and the man reached the camp entrance, I heard shouts in Spanish from my left. I refocused and locked the 3D cameras and took up the handheld. I panned it to the left to the southwest tunnel while adding slow zoom.

The vehicle was a Jeep. Soldiers in uniforms I didn't recognize walked alongside it. There was an officer present—I could tell he was in charge by his aggressive voice and pointing. I was widening the composition and minutely dialing in to zoom when the rain and the day were torn by gunfire. The muzzle flashes were coming from the soldiers alongside the Jeep. From my camera position back in the vegetation, I filmed the officer pointing and stepping back.

Gunfire also opened up to my right, two shots from a handgun. I panned the handheld to the camp entrance, the pan way too fast for viewing, and it filled with the spewing of bullets and tracer rounds tearing into the camp entry. I set the handheld down and took to the 3D viewfinder. My fellow Seabees and Specwars were scrambling for weapons.

The enemies were spraying the camp with automatic fire. The cruel cracking of the 50mm gun on the Jeep started. I filmed my team rising and falling as they were overpowered and consumed by gunfire. The businessman was cut in half, vertically, and blown farther into the camp entrance. I filmed Dirks exploding backward with both his weapon and most of his head taking flight. There was a total of four muzzle flashes from the camp.

I zoomed so that the camp entrance filled the frame. A very brave Madera crashed through the foliage from the right side of the composition. He took three steps out into the rain and the clearing, firing his machine gun into the vegetation where enemy soldiers were making a flanking attack. His weapon was still spraying when bullets destroyed his chest. He was knocked off his feet, and all gunfire stopped.

I switched the 3D cameras off. Scrambling farther into the trees and overgrowth, I knelt and hid. My hands were trembling. I was gulping air in a useless attempt to calm down, my mind was a blur of violent and bloody images. There was no understanding. The madness had been so sudden, so vicious, and so deadly.

The Jeep drove up the airstrip, and the officer entered the camp alone, his sidearm drawn. He fired the gun one time before coming back out to the Jeep. Climbing into the passenger seat, the vehicle made a U-turn and drove back up the airstrip and disappeared into the southwest tunnel.

I remained hidden in the trees and greenery back from the cameras. I needed to check on the others in the camp but couldn't will my legs to move. Perhaps I was in shock, I don't know. The gunfight I had witnessed was a movie gone off its tracks like some *hack* director had lobbed a grenade into a love scene.

Kneeling in the dank soil and bush, I watched the opening to the camp. There was no movement, no voices. Hours passed. The rain clouds rolled away. The hot sun sank into the trees.

When night fell, a group of soldiers reentered the airfield from the south. Lanterns lit, they took up a position halfway to the camp chattering and laughing in Spanish.

Somewhere in the night, a cry of anguish carried from our camp. I needed to get to whoever it was, to help in any way I could. I stood, preparing to circle to the camp through the vegetation. A lantern crossed the field followed by a rifle crack. The moaning ended.

I was trapped in a fever for revenge mixed with the need to survive. The lantern remained in the camp moving here and there. I willed it to leave, for all the killers to return from where they had come. The hours passed. With each hour, the silence from my fellow soldiers weighed heavy on my heart.

At sunrise, the Jeep and troops retreated. I unloaded the cameras and ran across the airstrip.

Everyone was dead, disfigured by bullet holes. I covered the bodies of the Seabee's and Specwars with sections of tent canvas and placed a heavy stone on each of their chests.

I packed the film cans and a few MREs inside two shoulder duffels adding six of the phosphorus flares and my transistor radio. I spent the rest of the day hidden in the vegetation waiting for nightfall. Fitful sleep captured me for short spells in the heat and humidity under clouds of insects.

When the moon rose, I traversed down the mountain. On the first big turn in the trail, I stepped out onto the landing. It was more like a balcony. I lit a flare and set it upright with rocks before continuing down the trail. I did the same on the next three balconies and was on the beach two hours later.

I ate without interest, no matter how long it had been, one bland MRE after another. At the entrance to the beach from the trail, I set up a trip line. I dug a pit in the trees and lay down inside with my duffels pulled over most of my body. The rest of that night was endless and torn by images of faces and bodies hideously ripped open by bullets. Nodding off occasionally, I fought to end the movie-like stream of faces no longer young and hopeful, replaced by blood-stained cruelty.

I woke to the sweeping of searchlights on the beach and the hushed run of dinghies onto the shore.

Scene 10

Instead of a survivor's welcome, I was quickly handcuffed and whisked away in one of the dinghies out to the transport ship offshore. My goggles were confiscated, and I was ordered to shower and shave. I was given a new set of blues and boots before being placed in the brig down in the ship's hold. The cell was a steel cage. I was fed and told I would be uncuffed and allowed to sleep after interrogation.

The first interrogation was brief—no more than an hour of questioning. I was abandoned for a few hours but still in handcuffs. The second round of questioning was longer, and four new officers attended. Their focus was on the contents of the film cans. It was clear to me that they had developed and viewed the footage.

The ship set sail some days later. It was hard to tell time down below. Twice a day, I was escorted to the bathroom and fed. I was also allowed a brief shower every third day.

"Why am I being held like this?" I asked time and again.

"For your own good," was the common reply.

The last time I asked, the sailor escorting me said, "You were part of something you shouldn't have been. They're not sure what to do with you."

I stopped asking.

As best I could count, we were at sea for eighty-one days.

When we reached land, the ship was moored in a harbor, and I was transferred to shore in a launch with two armed guards. I was moved to a military brig on the base and informed that a tribunal was being arranged. My handcuffs were removed, and my new cell had a sink and toilet and a sliding shelf from which I received my meals.

By my count, I received the box of personal belongings ninety-four days later. Inside was my transistor radio and my goggles. Having my vision returned to me was a relief. I put the radio up on the narrow sill under the barred window and wished I had fresh batteries. Days later, I was allowed an envelope, a piece of paper, and the stub of a pencil. I wrote to Ira, asking about Pierce and Hilda. I never received a reply. I was allowed to send a letter every ten days and did so. I continued to ask Ira about my son and if there was anything he could do to secure my release.

I remained in custody for ten months and was escorted to hearings on three occasions. There were lengthy, vague discussions and decisions made. I felt confused in the makeshift sunlit courtrooms in front of the small group of officers. I was rarely addressed directly. It came to me that I was viewed as a pawn that they were trying to place, to hide, on a much more important and complicated board.

After a series of brain scans, the doctors started me on a regimen of psychiatric treatments. I suspect the new medications were the reason I started seeing glowing clouds around other people. In particular, about their heads. I had no choice but to abandon my goggles and set them up on the windowsill beside my transistor radio. Wearing the goggles expanded the glowing light into solid blocks around the heads of those I looked at. I was ordered to put them on a few times during neurological treatments and was questioned about my weaving walk. I explained that I was trying to avoid colliding with each person's blockish aura.

Living within the 2D world made my confinement a bit easier. I began to appreciate my small, gray cell and the lack of confusing colors. Even though I still couldn't see human eyes, at least the glows were muted and not boxlike. The soldiers I saw in the halls and hearings had different hues, and it took me awhile to sort them out. Eventually, I assigned good or bad intentions and attitudes to the varying shades. Most people I encountered had a blend of colors, conflicting tints, and shades. A very small number had a smooth and calm glow of cream and gold.

Near the end of my confinement, I returned to my cell from showering, and there stood Lieutenant Ezra Mayer waiting for me. His aura was a new and interesting blend—a sky blue with a core of pulsing purple. He gestured for me to sit beside him on my bunk. I noted the manila folder on his lap. He squeezed my shoulder as I sat, and I watched the purple expand when he removed his hand.

A guard entered the cell through the door that had been left open for the first time. He set my satchel on the edge of the bunk and left without a word. His glow was like most—conflicted and bored. I turned to Ezra and looked straight at his nose and mouth.

"Two items, BB. First, I'm not here. Second, the failed rescue mission never occurred. You've been what they're describing as deranged. For nearly two years. If you agree to a Section 8, you're going to be drummed out of the service."

There was a hazy pearl of shimmering black beginning to appear within the center of his glow.

"Well?" he asked.

"Well?"

"Do you agree?"

I looked away from his head to the windowsill. "Yes, sir."

"Good choice. It's going to take a few days to process you out. Quite a few more days of train trips to get you back to Hollywood."

I was studying my transistor radio beside my goggles.

"Sir," I said. "I heard her."

"Who would that be, son?"

"Mumm."

His head followed my gaze at the windowsill. The black pearl glow was receding, and the purple expanded. He stood and took the radio down.

"Recently?" he asked.

"No," I answered. "When I was on the mountaintop. The airstrip."

"Oh. Yes. On your mission. That never took place. You've had two years of madness. I'm told you experienced many odd visions."

I turned to him and watched the black glow expand.

"Does it matter that your discharge status will be...murky?" he asked.

"I'm sorry? Oh. No, sir. That's fine."

"That must have been quite a blow."

"Sir? Mumm's voice was..."

"When you took that fall."

He read the confusion in my expression.

"You fell off the ladder. In Archives. You slipped and landed head first."

"Sir?"

"Don't remember, do you? That's best."

His head was aimed at his hands. He pointed to the empty battery compartment on the back of the transistor radio.

"Is it coming clear to you?" he asked. "Civilian radio reception? In a jungle two thousand miles from the States."

The black aura had consumed all of his head.

"Brain damage can be mysterious and strange."

I looked away from him.

"I'd like to see my son," I said quietly.

"You will. And soon."

He stood.

"I'd say 'so long,' but I'm not here." And with that, he left.

I opened the satchel and found the clothing I had worn when I enlisted—my black suit and shoes, my white shirt and green tie. Pushed into the lower-left corner of the bag were my letters to Ira minus the postage I had been promised.

ACT SIX
HOLLYWOOD

Jar
To cause a short, tremulous motion of, to cause to tremble, as by a sudden shock or blow; to shake; to shock; as, to jar the earth; to jar one's faith.

<u>Scene 11</u>

Ira picked me up at the train depot in his new convertible. I rode home in the back seat with my darling Pierce laughing and talking at my side. He had my old Tewe director's lens in his hands. He asked for my goggles, put them on, and stuck his head out the window and into the wind. His eight-year-old glow was a complex plaid of orange and green.

"BB..." Ira spoke to me over his shoulder. I admired the steady cream and gold that encircled the back of his head.

"So you're prepared, you have two new adopted children. Twins."

• • • •

I SPENT my first season—winter—poolside with my three children, Hilda, and Ira. My two new children, the twins, were named Jared and Baby Ruth. They were two years younger than Pierce. I spent most of that winter watching the three of them play and converse. The twins lived in

Mother's tall and imposing mansion. Pierce and I continued in the guest-house. Hilda told me she had asked Mother where Jared and Baby Ruth came from and was met with a wall of silence. One of Mother's assistants brought me the final adoption documents to sign.

During that period, I stopped taking the prescriptions for my "neurological injury," and the glows went away. After the holidays, Ira got me shoehorned in at Lion Heart Pictures.

The former Dashing Nash Movies had been resurrected and renamed. Businessmen and executives I rarely saw owned the studio. I was assigned a rewrite of a script titled *Chuck's Big Mistake*. Another writer was doing the dialogue, and I was told to focus on settings, scenes, and situations. The memo I received ordered me to "add spice and explosive turns of fate."

Chuck's Big Mistake was a hit, especially with the targeted teenage audience. Chuck's sidekick in that film was elevated to costar in the follow-up, *The Misadventures of Chuck & Coots.*

As before, I worked on the third installment while the second was produced. We were gifted by a visit to the writing office by the executives. As a team, we were thanked for helping the studio "find and strike the vein."

After what I had experienced in my short life, working in comedy was foreign to me. What I had a knack for was providing unexpected and dangerous twists to be overcome—like tossing lit dynamite into a dining room scene. I was constantly reminded by memo to add "surprises that throw audiences back in their seats."

Some of the misadventures were easy for me to come up with. Pierce and the twins provided what I thought were comical situations and material to expand on. Most of their poolside play centered on making adventure and rescue movies. I would write and sketch and take the pages to Lion Heart where the film's trajectory was predetermined—another rescue story with many pratfalls as the incompetent and, I suppose, humorous Chuck and Coots pursued a lovely actress through a haunted mansion. Most of my odd and dangerous twists were included in the scripts. The fourth C&C film, *Chuck & Coots at War,* worked the same vein—rescue and slapstick. This time, the film was set in the Army with the primary location in a foreign, tropical war zone.

While number four was in preproduction, the screenplay needing only minor rewrites, I began an independent story and screenplay. The working title was *Pain Staking,* and I was given the green light to work on it part-time because of the continued success of the C&C films. What I held back from my fellow writers and the executives was the intended return of 3D. I studied and adopted the once-failed camera-as-character approach based on my interest and delight in the film *The Lady in the Lake.* My script for *Pain Staking* was largely void of dialogue for the main character, an escaped felon. The script was green-lighted for Coots, whose star had eclipsed Chuck's.

The escaped felon first crosses wide-open country to an abandoned silver mine high up on a mountain. There's a ghost town and a narrow row of buildings. The felon searches the buildings assembling clues to a mystery the audience doesn't yet grasp. He is stressed and worried by the authorities hot on his trail. He can see them far down the mountain, their train of vehicles climbing the winding roads dragging up dust clouds. He devises ways to slow their approach including placing dynamite from the mine on the bridge with the plunger set under a board. The felon begins to search for the elderly, rogue US marshal who has hidden a kidnapped woman somewhere in the camp town. It's the woman the felon is trying to rescue. The authorities are continuing up the mountain from the east and, as the clock ticks, he searches for the girl, finding clues. The felon attacks the marshal and is injured. He carries on, wounded and pressed for time.

Alongside the incomplete script in my typewriter were the storyboards that showed the trolley paths for the cameras which would be the felon's eyes through the story.

During that year, three of us were assigned to writing a space-adventure script, C&C five rewrites, and segments of a madman-on-an-airplane film. *Pain Staking* languished at times. Other days, it was encouraged and supported, the difference in studio attitude being the company's financial status and my link to the continued success of the C&C movies.

The love for the Chuck and Coots movies turned sour with number five. We were told that the proceeds were disappointing, that the "vein has been played out."

Pain Staking went into preproduction. I was told that the script and camera format were risky and odd enough to make it either a surprise hit or an expensive crash and burn.

• • • •

WHEN WORK allowed, I spent my evenings poolside with Pierce, Jared, and Baby Ruth. The three of them were like little birds and had a way of play that kept me grinning. Pierce often directed their activities. Jared was attentive, smiling, and distant. Baby Ruth clearly adored her twin brother and was a constant beside him, the two head-to-head in their private and merry conversations. During the evening pool parties, Hilda would enjoy a respite with her magazines at the umbrella table when Ira wasn't with her. It pleased me to see the affection that Hilda and Ira had developed. They, like Jared and Baby Ruth, appeared to have their own language and wavelength.

The children's play was mostly movie making—Pierce with his Tewe director's lens and his siblings as his cast and crew. The three of them dreamed up plots in between swims, sitting on their beach towels, and crunching and sucking on popsicles. Pierce directed, speaking in his crisp voice under the black circle of the round Tewe lens. Other times, Pierce would wander off with the lens and film the garage, our guest house, or the clouds while the twins talked in soft voices in their smiling, private world. I enjoyed the contrast between Pierce's red hair and freckles and the tan skin and black hair of Jared and Baby Ruth.

Ira and Hilda and I were sitting on another warm, golden evening when I realized my brain had changed. I was studying Jared's face. He was focused on what Baby Ruth was whispering, his steady, intelligent expression locked on her. The change had come suddenly.

There were his delicate and lovely eyelashes. It had been years since I had been able to see this way—this completely, this deeply.

There was a crack and splash—my water glass hitting the pool deck.

The clean, white circles around chocolate colored windows revealed Jared's fine intelligence and personality.

I could see his eyes.

"BB?" Ira tried to stir me.

I waved him away and stared, fearful that my new son's eyes would dissolve into the usual smooth skin I had seen for so long. I watched humor brighten in them as Baby Ruth rolled back laughing.

Hilda scratched her chair back, standing to help clean up the glass. I didn't move. Jared's nose crinkled upward accenting the delight in his gaze, and he turned away from his sister. He looked across the lawn between us and aimed his beautiful, lively eyes to mine. His expression went neutral. Baby Ruth was giggling and pedaling her bare feet to the sky. Hilda was at my knees picking up pieces of glass. Jared and I continued to look deep into one another without so much as a blink.

"BB?" Ira said.

Jared's face relaxed, and his expression was peaceful and knowing. Baby Ruth bumped his shoulder, and his stare continued. That darling and handsome boy. He raised one of his hands and waved gently. I began to raise mine. Pierce yelled from the pool, and Jared let out a sideways smile. Then something wonderful happened—Jared winked at me.

He turned to Pierce and yelled back as he took Baby Ruth's chubby hand. Pierce slid the director's lens aside to bark a direction, and there were his wide, sweet, amused eyes. I studied him while he yelled across the water to Baby Ruth telling her to sit up and scoot away from Jared. Pierce's eyes were an amazing blue-gray. He stood chest deep in the warm pool water waiting patiently and watching his siblings from the side of his lens. There was relief in his eyes when Baby Ruth did as directed. I followed the aim of the raised lens to Baby Ruth's lovely, tan face and saw that her eyes were sleepy and cocoa colored—and watching Jared closely.

I heard Hilda say, "BB, please move so I can sweep."

Ira said, "We have a production meeting at 8:00 a.m."

I turned in my chair, carefully, and slid it back from Hilda's broom and dustpan, giving all my focus to the three children, my three young ones.

The sun set, and we all stayed poolside illuminated by the aqua lights from the water and candles glowing on the umbrella table. Ira and Hilda had taken each other's hands and held on tenderly. The children sat in a triangle on their colorful beach towels sharing a bowl of saltines. Ira talked softly about the progress on *Pain Staking*.

On a night of such surprise, grace, and wonder, we all stayed within our usual roles and patterns of conversation. Hilda nudged the three children into saying their good nights to one another before she gathered Pierce's beach towel and his lens. I received a brushing good-night kiss from Pierce and told him I would be back to the guesthouse in a few. Gathering up Jared and Baby Ruth's damp towels and the saltines bowl, I walked with them from the pool area and along the garden path to Mother's mansion which was lit from all the second-story windows and balconies. Music and many voices carried from above the garden doors. I stopped at the edge of the brush brick patio. Jared and Baby Ruth headed to the door to the dark first story. Like the nights before, I waited until one of Mother's assistants appeared from the shadows and took both of my children's hands. She turned with them, silently. Jared let himself be led a few steps before he locked his knees and turned. Looking over his shoulder, he winked at me again under the falling wave of his jet-black hair.

• • • •

CASTING CHANGES for *Pain Staking* occurred as different opinions and money concerns were worked out. The director, Mr. Stephens, had his own ideas and passions. He'd had a string of successes before the big war and during the conflict with his newsreels. Mr. Stephens adjusted the script and storyboards, dialogue, and crew selection. Ira was thankfully kept on as the 3D cinematographer.

When filming began, I wasn't invited to the set. Those days were spent in the narrow writers' office in the building across from Soundstage Four. From time to time, I was told to dash over to transcribe revisions, mostly changes to the visual design. I was allowed to stand in the back of the screening room during dailies but was seldom noticed or called upon. *Pain Staking* was no longer my film as it morphed into Mr. Stephens's property. He had his own vision and thematic concerns. The movie's story was lost on me by then, but I delighted in the main character's movements within the subjective 3D world and view.

With my involvement reduced, I was assigned to other projects and followed the progress of the *Pain Staking* production through conversations with Ira. My days became short, and my workload lightened, and the chatter among my fellow writers in our skinny office was that if the film hung, so would I.

During those summer weeks, Los Angeles and the Hollywood enclave were encased in a heat wave, a row of days in a hundred-degree swelter under hazy, white skies. I was home one midweek afternoon waiting for Pierce to find his swimsuit, looking forward to another pool party with his brother and sister. I gazed out our guesthouse door to Mother's mansion higher up on the hill and squinted from the sweat on my brow. Two days prior, I had noted that the pool water had turned and needed chemicals and a leaf net sweeping. Standing there, I saw that the lawn was fading to yellow and needed mowing. Pierce ran past me from the guesthouse dragging his beach towel and grasping his director's lens close to his chest. The patio doors of Mother's stately home opened and released Jared and Baby Ruth. The first floor was dark as usual. The balcony doors and windows of the second story were lit.

I turned my attention to the antics of my three kids. Jared entered the pool area carrying his sailboat, a gift from me on the twins' recent birthday. The three were going to continue their ocean adventure movie. He carried the foot-long wooden sailboat close to his chest, and when his thoughtful eyes looked at it, I saw sadness. The boat was missing its mast and had been nearly broken in half.

"Mother came into my room while I was asleep," he said, as though that was explanation enough.

Hilda appeared from behind Jared and his sister, with one arm draped in colorful towels and a beach bag over her shoulder. She held a snack bowl in her free hand. Behind her, the patio doors remained open, and I got my first glimpse of the Doc and the Blonde, as Hilda described them, standing half in sunlight with their chests and faces in the shadows. Hilda had explained that the two had taken up residence in the mansion on the same day Jared and Baby Ruth arrived. This couple looked down at us until Hilda followed Jared and Baby Ruth onto the pool deck. When the double glass patio doors closed, I turned my attention to my three.

On the Sunday morning three days later, I was summoned to Mother's mansion. I answered the telephone in the kitchen in the guesthouse reaching over from the small table where Pierce and Ira were dismantling and studying a 16mm camera.

The voice on the line was a man's, and I decided it was the Doc, the only male member of the household that I knew of.

"Your wife would like to speak to you," he said.

Hearing "wife," I paused. There had never been a marriage. Before I could say anything, the call clicked off.

The grounds were looking worse for wear, wilted from the current heat wave. Past the garden, the planters on the large patio held sun-fried, crisp, dead flowers. A lounge for sunbathing lay on its side and the outdoor dining tables and chairs were pushed this way and that. The brush bricks were littered with dead leaves, dust, and flotsam.

Before me was the back entrance to Mother's imposing and once well-kept palatial residence. That was no more—the mansion looked tired and neglected. Peeling paint and unwashed windows. An overflowing garbage can was next to a haphazard stack of storage boxes. There were two mounds of castaway clothing, broken sections of wallboard, and worn, abandoned furniture.

I entered the big room for the first time in years. The floors, walls, and ceiling had been repainted, and the furniture had new fabric. The primary color was a green covered with fine, snakelike ribbons of salmon pink. Dirty glasses and plates of dried, wrinkled food lay everywhere. I wove through the couches and low tables of the first room and entered the second, which swept out to the right, to the southern draped windows on the far side of the dining area. The third large room to the left included the foyer and entry hall. There were at least two weeks of mail on the green tiles under the mailbox slot beside the front doors. I walked around to the base of the stairs. The steps were stained from spills and needed vacuuming. The air was stale and unpleasant, and it reeked of burned food and medicinal or, less likely, cleaning supplies.

Halfway up the stairs, a door opened on the landing. I looked up through the banister posts. I stopped. An immense woman in an ill-fitting Hawaiian dress stepped to the rail. She wore a telephone headset, and the cloth cord trailed her very large, bare feet. She held a silver tray in her over-inflated hands and looked at me with mild surprise.

"Who are you? No. What are you doing in the house?" Her soft and playful voice contrasted with the scowl on her fat, creased face.

Before I could reply, another door opened from the left side of the landing, and the blonde walked into view.

"Go plug in and get back to work," she told the large woman, who nodded her downcast head, her three chins bobbing.

"I'm here to see Mother," I said to the blonde. She was wearing a white cotton dress that resembled a nurse's uniform. Her expression was hostile and stern.

"She changed her mind," she said firmly. She extended a thick, blue folder to me. I climbed the remaining steps between us.

"I wrote out her instructions," she said, handing me the packet. "Her needs." She added.

I scanned the other doors wondering which ones belonged to Jared and Baby Ruth. Something nudged my knuckles, and I looked down. The blonde was handing me a pen. All the doors looked the same except the ornate carved double doors at the end of the landing, painted a baby pink—it had to be the entrance to Mother's room.

The blonde cleared her throat.

I was trying to imagine Jared and Baby Ruth living in this place of stale air, filth, and silence.

"Leave."

I wanted to ask for a quick look inside the kid's rooms, but I didn't. Her tone and posture turned me around, and I went downstairs. I was about to leave the mansion when I was drawn to a side door with a brass kick plate.

It was a large kitchen more like that of a restaurant than a house. There were two of everything—refrigerators, freezers, stoves, and ovens. There was a long worktable under hanging pots and pans and cutlery. Everywhere I looked, the surfaces were distraught with old food and unwashed dinnerware and clutter. Sitting on a tall chair before the left sink, I opened the latticed blinds and sprayed the blue folder in sunlight. I opened it and flipped through the many pages, signing my name beside every red underline. I gave the documents enough attention to see that I was authorizing the sale of the mansion which, like our prior homes, was in my name.

Underneath the sales contract was a common-law marriage agreement. It was already filled in and had a notarized seal from the state of North Carolina. All that was missing was my signature. I paused, pen in hand. I hadn't seen Mother in several years. A long time ago, I had rescued her. Maybe the marriage would make her feel safe? Perhaps thaw her heart? I didn't know. I signed the agreement.

Looking out the grimy kitchen window and down the hill, I saw the sparkling, blue wavering water of the swimming pool. I was distracted by the smell of burned and rotted food, so I took the folder with me out into the fresh air.

• • • •

THE NEXT morning, Hilda collected Pierce to drive him to school, and I went off to put my smoking, blue automobile in the repair shop. After a short day in the writers' office, mostly working on rewrites to the space-adventure film, I took the bus to pick up my car. The tall, old man in green coveralls had diagnosed the motor. It was terminal. He gave me the price for a replacement, and I took the bus home, not approving the repairs because I didn't have the money.

Pierce had figured out the lawn mower and had it fueled and running. As he mowed the overgrown, yellow lawn, Jared and I went into the cool shade of the garage. We read the sides of the pool chemical buckets and began our first experiment to remove the mossy green from the pool water.

Pierce finished the lawns and rolled the mower to the garage and returned from the guesthouse with his rebuilt 16mm movie camera. He walked down into the pool with his shoes and clothes on which made Baby Ruth laugh. She was sitting beside Hilda who was reading her magazines. The day before, the three kids had filmed the sinking of the sailboat. Jared climbed into the pool wearing a torn-up white shirt with ash smudges on the sides of his handsome face. He was carrying a broken board. He swam to the deep end and, at Pierce's direction, treaded water with the board across his chest.

Baby Ruth left the table and kneeled on the pool deck. She watched Jared closely over Pierce's shoulder and the raised camera.

"Quiet!" Pierce barked.

Jared squinted, and his expression changed to bewildered and determination.

The pool area was silent. Everyone was focused on Jared's plight. I felt Hilda's hand on my wrist, but I didn't turn.

Pierce called over his shoulder, "Baby Ruth. Please."

As rehearsed, Baby Ruth hefted a section of plywood taken from the garage and pushed it into the water. She entered the pool and placed her hands out wide on the wood.

"Roll on four," Pierce directed.

Baby Ruth began shoving and pulling on the plywood causing a series of waves that quickly reached Jared.

"Action."

Jared took a mouthful of water and choked and gagged and turned away. As scripted, he spoke a single word to the view of the vast ocean.

"Sharks."

He went wide-eyed but kept the resolute set to his jaw as he floundered in the waves, looking back and forth and side to side for the predators. His expression was torn with shock and pain just before he was pulled under. One of his hands remained on the rocking piece of wood.

Pierce called "cut" and leaned around the raised camera.

Baby Ruth stopped making waves.

A voice, angry and familiar, bellowed from the garden up the hill. "You! Husband!"

I waited until Jared reappeared and winked at his brother before I turned around.

Mother wore a lime, translucent robe that draped down along the sides of her naked body. She had put on weight since I had last seen her. Her belly and her breasts were plump and pale and ghostly white. The hair on her mound and head looked like cotton candy and were dyed a vibrant snow-white. Her lips were painted a glossy pink, and she wore black sunglasses.

I realized that I was staring instead of answering.

Her hands went to her hips, and her breasts bounced when she called down.

"Where are the signed papers?"

The kids were wide-eyed and as stunned as I was to see Mother in daylight. I heard Hilda's magazines spill and slap the concrete. I got up from the umbrella table and went to our guesthouse where the blue folder lay on the small table within the sprawl of camera parts and 3D reels and viewers.

Carrying the documents up the paths to the landing where she stood, I studied the open lime-colored robe parted like a curtain. I had never seen her naked before. I felt a rare mix of emotions—lust and loss.

"I signed everything," I stammered, handing over the folder.

Her pale, lovely fingers flipped through the pages, confirming the signatures. Satisfied, she turned for the darkness of the house.

"Maybe you and I and the children could celebrate?" I said to her back.

Her voice carried from the shadows beyond the door.

"Not going to happen. You might've saved me, but I'm not part of your collection."

• • • •

WHEN *PAIN Staking* bombed, I was unexpectedly credited with most of the movie, both inside Lion Heart Pictures and in the hastily edited newspaper advertisements. My workdays became shorter. The space-adventure film was in trouble, and I was told to work on sequencing and continuity as filming continued. The movie was bogging down as it tried to carry the airship romance *and* the trials of space travel. I took red ink to the long, anguished break-up scenes and penned a single shot of a letter the main character finds at the helm. He opens it, reacts, and gets back to repairing the turbo thrusters. Four minutes cut to thirty-seven seconds.

Twelve days into the shoot, Ira entered the writers' office and sat down beside my desk near the back of the narrow room.

"Don't murder the mailman," he told me. He had a sheet of paper in his hand which was covered with columns of numbers. "They chose me, I suppose because we're buddies. To the quick, you're fired."

•   •   •   •

I SPENT four weeks going through the trades and newspapers and typing up resumes on the typewriter the studio had given me as a parting gift. I began to worry about money each time I opened a packet of cash. Mother's expenses continued to come my way and, while reduced by her dwindling number of employees, the packets were thinning every week.

Six weeks after my dismissal, I received a telephone call at the guest-house—an invitation to an interview with Legend Pictures. The caller explained that the company wasn't a studio but a production house that was using military newsreels and archived footage to build historical shorts for sale to grade schools, community colleges, and collectors.

My screenplay skills were not required. The position was for a member of the editing team. I accepted the offer and planned to take the bus to the office in downtown Hollywood the following Friday.

On one of the days in between, Hilda pulled me aside while the kids shared a bowl of watermelon at the umbrella table. I hadn't been able to pay her the past two weeks, and she had a solution. Later that same afternoon, Ira and I unlocked the second guesthouse, and while it aired out, we cleaned it and made it nice for Hilda. She liked the idea of living there rent-free in exchange for caring for my three. That same day, Hilda told me that Jared and Baby Ruth would no longer be sleeping in the mansion but with her in her new place. I'm not sure if the twins were more excited or relieved.

That Friday, I was right on time at Legend Pictures. When I arrived, there were already six other applicants sitting in the untidy front office, leaving me to stand. I completed the necessary paperwork and waited forty-five minutes before the secretary read my name and nodded to the adjoining door.

The interview room was dingy and cluttered with old screening equipment, projectors, and splicing machines. There were two metal chairs and a wooden table. Across from me sat Mr. Nash—the director of Mumm's and my film, *Savior,* and my previous employer in the delivery business.

He used the intercom on the table to speak to the secretary, "Let those others go."

He gestured to the chair opposite his and opened a file with my name written on it.

"I saw your name and had to wonder." His welcoming smile froze. "We've got a history, of sorts."

I agreed.

"No filming here, Danser. Our angle is mining the miles of old newsreel footage for repackaging." He set my resume down on the table. "Appears you have a knack for speeding up storylines. Are you interested?"

"Yes."

"Good. In six weeks, we'll have completed the acquisition of film stocks and be ready to go. You'll start one week early to learn our edit and splice machines."

"Five weeks?" I asked. "I was hoping..."

The frosty smile stretched. "Short on cash?"

"Yes."

He opened the center desk drawer and took out a set of car keys on a black fob. "If you're interested in returning to the delivery business, I can pay up front. Cash. Starting tonight."

The keys were dangling from his fingers.

"It comes with a car like before. With the same cleaning and garaging rules. I'll have the car's title put in your name. For our own reasons."

The telephone on the desk rang. He ignored it. It jingled three times before being replaced by a small blinking light.

"Like before, you'll be given the addresses the night of. You'll also deliver small bags with the...*employees.*"

Mr. Nash selected a button on the telephone and spoke to someone without pause or listening. He ended the call and rose from the table.

"For tonight, my secretary has the addresses for you. Starting tomorrow, you'll get calls at your number. Is your telephone still working?"

"I believe so."

"Do this. She's going to pay you for tonight. Go down to Pacific Bell and pay your bill. Pay it forward, too."

I agreed.

"You'll like the car." He walked to the door and opened it. "It's a '61 Lincoln."

I took the keys, and he closed the door at my heels. The secretary gave me a note with the addresses and an envelope half full of cash.

That night, after my three were bunked out in Hilda's place, I backed the dirty Lincoln from the garage and went to work.

I made deliveries almost every night during the five weeks before reporting to work at Legend Pictures. As before, most of the employees I delivered to the wealthy homes were stylishly dressed and chatty. Later in the wee hours, these same young women were disturbed, unraveled, and drugged. Sometimes they were incoherent as I drove them to their apartments. Occasionally, the employees were young men who also went through the before and after Jekyll and Hyde mutation.

I found my role in this business distasteful. These young women were being drained of all hope and life. Like them, the constant need for money kept me at it.

During those days, regardless of what I did each night, I enjoyed my three. When they were home from their schools, we lived in the pool area with laughter coming from all corners and the open doors of the two guesthouses.

A week before I was supposed to start at Legends, I turned the black Lincoln into the driveway and saw a sandwich board on the south corner sidewalk before the mansion. It didn't have "For Sale" written on it, which would have been indiscreet for that neighborhood, but the sign—

with only a telephone number—made the intention clear. I asked Hilda if she heard anything. She hadn't, so I filed the question away.

· · · ·

ON MY first day at Legend Pictures, I wore my black suit, white shirt, and green tie and stood out on the street, in the day's early heat, waiting for the office to open. I was on time, early, in fact, ready to start at 8:00 a.m. I was curious about what genre of film I would be working on and what kind of editing equipment I was going to learn.

The street was busy, so I waited in the alcove before the front door. The cracked tiles were dusty and covered with bits of litter. My black shoes and cuffs were tan by 9:00 a.m. I knocked on the front door again as I'd done four times over the past hour. No reply nor movements or voices.

At 9:15 a.m., I stepped out on the sidewalk and looked in through Legend's front window. The blinds were drawn. At 10:00 a.m., I gave the front door three strong knocks, waited, and tried the door handles. They were locked.

That night, I drove the Lincoln to the donut shop to get the to-and-from addresses for the night's employee. I asked the man with the list and the small bag of medical bottles if he knew anything about Legend being closed for the day.

"For the day?" he chuckled. "Try *for the decade*. No. Better yet, try *for like permanent*. Crazy Nash and his grab-the-cash schemes."

So began the days when I only worked nights, and, while glad to have that cash, I worried even more about money.

Mother's mansion remained on the market for the remainder of 1962 without a single offer. The front of the property became overgrown and brown from lack of care. The boys and I kept up the backside of the property—we watered and mowed the lawn, and Jared and I found the correct mixture of chemicals and treatments to keep the pool clean and clear. The delivery business money was almost enough to cover our living expenses, but I couldn't stay afloat in the waves of bills from the mansion.

As the packets of cash dwindled, I began another search in the industry papers for studio employment, typing resumes on the old Underwood and mailing them off one by one.

Sometimes there were no replies, and other times the resumes came back stamped "Return to Sender." When the telephone was shut off for nonpayment, I drove the black Lincoln to the telephone company and worked out a deal for a small amount of cash in exchange for restored service. I needed to pay the water company and power bill but couldn't.

That afternoon, when Hilda brought the children home from school, Pierce had a note stating that he needed testing and eyeglasses. Another expense and an important one. At 5:00 p.m., the power company shut off the electricity. Ira was kind enough to loan me enough to cover the bill, but I passed on turning the power back in favor of covering grocery expenses.

There were three packets of cash remaining in the satchel that I kept in the closet Pierce and I shared. Our meager savings went quickly, the packets thinning even with my delivery job income.

Two weeks later, a single packet was all that was left. I walked to the front of Mother's mansion and wrote down the telephone number for the realtor and called him. He confirmed that there had been no offers.

"That property needs a proper cleaning and restoration and repairs to make it marketable."

"Yes," I agreed. "There's no money for that. How about we lower the price?"

At that, he laughed and said, "Can't."

"Why?"

"With all those loans, the seconds, thirds, fourths, and fifths, you have very little wiggle room on the list price. Any chance you can get your wife to agree to a sizable downsize? To a less desirable zip code."

I didn't know anything about the loans.

"You want, I'll make the listing changes, but you'd better talk to your wife about the realities of your...situation. Might also want to take her pen and checkbook away from her if you don't mind me suggesting."

"How much house could we afford if we lower the price enough to sell?"

"Well, Mr. Danser, it will be a surprise. And not a pleasant one, especially for your wife. Why don't you come over to the office?"

•　•　•　•

I DROVE the Lincoln into town. The realtor set out a blue-lined notebook and a selected a pen.

"If you like, I'll draw up the price adjustment and get the documents to you by the end of the week. Gives you time to discuss this with your missus."

I agreed. But I didn't speak to Mother about this. I felt compelled to act, to protect my three.

The documents arrived, and I signed them.

The mansion sat unwanted for two months without even a walk-through that I knew of.

I drove down to the realtor's office to discuss the situation.

"An open house would help." He shook his head. "But she'd have to be out of the residence for those days and times, and we both know that is not even *close* to being in the cards."

"I agree. Let's lower the price again," I said.

Long ago, I had saved Mother; rescued her. My need to continue to protect her was a question I couldn't answer.

•　•　•　•

FEELING THE pressure, a squeeze, for money, I opened the last packet on that chilly winter night before heading off to work in the dirty Lincoln. Kneeling in front of the closet and closing my satchel, I sensed a closing panic that stirred up a possible solution. It would mean being away from the boys and Baby Ruth for several days, but it could solve our current situation and likely make us solvent for quite some time.

I walked over to Hilda's and knocked on the door. After a minute, I heard movement from inside, and Ira answered rubbing the side of his face.

"BB? What's wrong? It's after midnight."

"Nothing's wrong. Is Hilda awake?"

"No. She's sleeping, like all the sane do," he said with a friendly smile. "What do you need? I can wake her if you like."

"No, that's okay. I need to be away for a bit. Probably a week. Maybe two. Not sure. Can she watch over the kids while I'm away?"

"Sure. I'll brave answering for her. Better that than disturb her dreams."

"Here." I handed him half of the money from the last packet. "That should be enough for expenses and the usual unexpected."

"Sure, BB," he replied, taking the thin stack of cash. "What are you up to?"

"I'm gonna go get some money. Will you thank Hilda for me?"

"Yes, of course. And your three will be fine. Call them when you can."

We exchanged a hug, and I went back to my place. I packed a bag of clothes and kissed the brow of my darling, sleeping Pierce. Before I headed off to work, I opened the Lincoln's trunk and placed a selection of tools inside behind the paper bags of police cash and medicine bottles.

I closed the trunk and stood briefly outside the garage, looking to the two guesthouses with my heart and hopes extended to my children. I hoped that my solution would work out and see us all in better living conditions soon.

• • • •

I LEFT the donut shop and drove to a bungalow on the east edge of Hollywood. The house was dark and stayed that way as I turned into the short and narrow driveway. A gentle rain was falling, and I waited in the Lincoln for the employee to notice the running headlights beside the small house.

Eventually, the side door opened, and a woman came out leaving the porch light off. It was not my job to question, but I wondered about her immediately. In the headlight beams, the stocky woman staggered to the car in day-labor clothes, no makeup, and a natty cap on her untamed hair. I'd never seen an *employee* like her before. She found her way in a stupor past the passenger door and opened the rear door. Leaning in on the burgundy upholstery, she nearly toppled over and didn't climb in. Instead, she looked over the seat and floorboards. Stepping back from the car, she weaved into the headlights and back inside the bungalow. I waited. I was curious about her, but most of my thoughts were on *my solution*, the steps needed, and the tasks required.

Ten minutes passed before the woman reappeared. A portly, short man in similar laborer clothing followed her. He was as unsteady on his feet as she was. They were both carrying heavy bundles. When they entered the headlights, I saw the blankets that covered their loads.

They placed the bundles in the back seat.

The man slurred, "Wait."

I did, watching the two of them go back inside. He reappeared and placed a smaller bundle on the back seat between the two blankets. He closed the rear door and disappeared inside the dark house.

I backed the Lincoln out onto the street nearly taking out two curbside garbage cans. I put the address note on the dash and steered under a streetlamp and took out the Thomas Guide. After finding the street and using my fingertip to help memorize the route, I looked into the back seat where the short bundles were washed in the streetlight. It looked like I might be delivering two dwarfs which was not as odd as it might seem. I reached back and took hold of the middle, smaller bundle that was ready to fall off the seat between the larger blanketed bodies. I placed it in my lap and carefully unwrapped the small blanket.

My first thought was of Baby Ruth, who might have owned one, but she was too old for dolls. This one was life-size, and its arms and face were dirty, its red hair was tangled, and it wore a blue-and-white dress.

I climbed out and opened the rear door and gently pulled the blanket away from the first mound on the seat. A sleeping little girl, perhaps five years old. I placed my face to her mouth. She was breathing. Her breath had a chemical smell that was familiar. Circling the Lincoln in the streetlight on that thin, residential street, I pulled the blanket back from the head of a second girl who looked a bit older than the other.

With the doll in my hand, I looked up the road. Houses pressed close together on both sides as far as the headlights reached. Thinking over my years of deliveries, I tried to remember a similar delivery, and I couldn't, and that pleased me. And helped me make a big, but easy decision.

Back behind the wheel, I placed the doll between the sedated little girls and started the Lincoln.

"You two game for a road trip?" I asked the rearview mirror getting the silent reply I expected.

By dawn, we had crossed the border from California into Nevada.

At noon, I pulled into a highway-side motel and rented a room. When I returned to the automobile with the room key, the girls were sitting up and watching me closely. I opened the rear passenger door and was greeted by the taller of the two.

"I'm Molly. This is April. Mister, I gotta pee."

I jingled the room key, and she smiled.

Inside the motel room, Molly went straight to the bathroom, and April took the chair by the window.

"Mister," she asked. "Can you get us something to drink? Maybe something to eat?"

"Of course."

"And maybe a toothbrush?"

The toilet was flushed, and Molly came into the room looking relieved.

"He's gonna feed us," April told her.

"Yeah? Good. No cheese on anything, please. Hate cheese."

I agreed, and April, the younger of the two, asked, "Is it okay if we shower while you go get food?"

Before I could answer, Molly pointed to my goggles and said, "Those are scary."

I took them off and pocketed them.

"Yes. Enjoy the shower while I'm gone. Take your time."

My eyes were closed, and I could feel one of the headaches coming on appearing first as a metallic taste from the back of my mouth. I smiled for their benefit and listened to them cross the room and close and lock the bathroom door.

• • • •

I RETURNED with a paper box. Three fish burgers—no cheese, three colas, and two toothbrushes and a little tube of paste. The girls were sitting side by side at the foot of the bed and turned in unison as I entered.

"Mister, can we?" April asked, pointing to the television.

"It's BB, please."

"What is?"

"My name."

"Your name is BB?"

Before I could confirm my name to April, Molly said, "Like the name. Didja remember about no cheese?"

"Yes, I did."

"Thank you, BB."

The girls ate fast and left no scraps. Not even the errant slices of lettuce in the paper wrapper. Sitting at the window table, I ate as well.

"Mister? Er, BB, can we ask you a favor?"

Before I could reply, Molly added, "Have you seen April's Baby Knucklehead?"

"The doll in a blue and white dress? Yes. She's still in the car. I'll go get it."

"Thank you, BB," both girls said with the cola cans at their chins.

Both wore black satin party dresses along with knee-high, black silk stockings and black leather heels. I paused at the door.

"Would you two like a change of clothing? Maybe something more comfortable?"

Their faces tightened, and they squeezed closer together at the foot of the bed.

"Never mind," I said.

I went out into the hot day and retrieved Baby Knucklehead who had fallen to the floorboard. Back inside the motel room, the girls were head-to-head in hushed conversation which stopped when they saw me and the doll in my hand. I gave Baby Knucklehead to April and sat down at the table. I studied my cola can while the two whispered to each other, eyes forward.

I interrupted them, saying the word, "Yes."

"Huh?" Molly asked.

"What, BB?" April chimed.

"You can watch the television."

"Really?"

"Nice!"

I've no idea what they watched, but they enjoyed the television the rest of the afternoon. I found myself nodding off, reclining as best as I could, and sleeping in the chair beside the window.

When I awoke, it was with a start. My eyes hurt, and my thoughts were fast and scattered. I scanned the room and saw Molly and April asleep at the foot of the bed in the gray glow of the television. When they awoke an hour later, it was close to 10:00 p.m. I encouraged them to use the restroom before we got back on the road.

• • • •

JUST BEFORE sunrise, I pulled off to fuel the Lincoln again and found a motel half a mile up the frontage road. We were on the outskirts of a town called Winnemucca on Highway 80. Inside the motel office, I bought a USA map and two little bottles of shampoo. I had clearly woken the night clerk who had me fill out a card after accepting cash for the room. On the "traveling with" line I wrote "my daughters."

Through most of the night, Molly and April had been quiet, and when rare, oncoming headlights passed, they looked to be sleeping. When the three of us and Baby Knucklehead were in our room, they stayed shoulder to shoulder on the floor before the television with their backs against the foot of the bed.

I told them I was going to shower and went out and got my clothes from the Lincoln. Entering the room, I pointed to the television.

"Saturday morning cartoons." I smiled.

They watched me closely as I crossed to the bathroom and closed the door. I clicked the lock louder than necessary. I showered and changed in the bathroom. When I came back into the room, the girls looked at me in my clothing and appeared relieved. I had changed into weekend clothes— khaki shorts and a white shirt with my black suit and shoes in my hand.

"You two ready for breakfast?" I asked.

They conversed before Molly said, "Yes. Please. No cheese, okay?"

I agreed. "Just a thought. I think I saw a store up the road. Might have swimsuits and summer clothes."

Their brows furrowed in unison. Molly pressed up against April.

"There's a swimming pool here," I went on, and the girls looked pleased and curious.

After breakfast, we walked to the swimming pool between the motel office and the parking lot. Molly and April swam and played in the pool while I slept on a lounge chair I dragged into the shade of a weathered, brown tree.

• • • •

BESIDES SWIMSUITS, I had bought four pairs of shorts and shirts for the girls. Back in the room an hour before sundown, the girls locked themselves in the bathroom with the new clothes and their little bottles of shampoo. Entering the front room, April told me they had draped their swimsuits for drying, and Molly was carrying their prior black clothing.

"Can we throw these away?" she asked.

"Of course."

"Use a pillowcase," April suggested. She started to climb onto the bed to grab a pillow but stepped back and circled and pulled it from the side. She removed the pillowcase and helped Molly push their clothes inside.

"Where?" April asked me.

"Garbage can." I smiled, and she did too.

"There's this." Molly pulled her hand from the pillowcase before pushing it into the wastebasket. She held a small paper bag. "I think this one is April's. I can get you mine if you like?"

"Let me see," I replied, already suspecting, but hoping I was wrong. Molly handed me the bag, and I watched her worried expression as I felt inside. My fingers touched a handkerchief wrapped around a little tin bottle.

"Want me to get mine, too?" she asked, looking sad and expecting disappointment.

"No, thank you," I answered as kindly as I knew how.

Her shoulders relaxed, and she went to April and took her hand and led her to the floor before the television.

"Mister BB? Can we?" Molly asked.

"Of course. Maybe there're more cartoons?"

"Too late in the day for those," Molly informed me. The television warmed up with the sounds of manic carnage and canned laughter.

It was the curiosity and a lack of foresight that led me to pull the handkerchief from the crinkled little bag and remove the tin bottle. I remember thinking about how many of these I had seen and delivered. I also recalled similar bottles and rags from my Seabee days. I wish I had reflected on what I had seen in the morning's after, but I didn't.

I watched my left hand twist the cap off. I watched my right hand place the handkerchief over the bottle mouth. I watched my left hand tip and spill moisture on the cloth. My right hand raised this to my nose and mouth.

• • • •

IT WAS perhaps the next day, but I could have easily lost two. I came to, squatting in the shower. The water was crisp and cold, and I wore a swimsuit and my black suit jacket and my green tie, which wasn't knotted but draped around my neck. I left the shower running and found my feet and walked dripping from the bathroom. The motel room was tidy, save a collection of Coke cans and a half-empty bottle of something called Ten High in the clutter on the table. I stared and blinked and realized after a minute that this was a different motel room. Next, I remembered the existence of Molly and April and saw that they were gone.

I sat on the side of the made-up bed and slowly pulled my damp upper clothes off—the suit jacket and green tie. I sat there in my bare feet and my new pair of swim trunks with flashes of memories, mostly discordant images playing. I felt regret and remorse flushing my entire body with heat.

There was a note written on a napkin on top of the television.

Mr. BB,

Thank you for being nice and letting us go swimming. You have been conked out. April and I got hungry and want to go home and borrowed dollars from you. I will pay you back.

Molly

I walked unsteadily to the bathroom and used a towel to dry my hair and upper body. I retrieved my socks and shoes from the shower pan and went back into the room. The television was glowing but silent, and I went to the door in search of the two little girls.

The Lincoln was parked on the far side of the lot all by itself. I saw it had been in a wreck. The right-side fender was crunched, and the tires were caked with dirt. The motel grounds didn't look familiar, and I felt a new fear—we had traveled. An eastern wind was blowing warm rain, and I walked the small motel grounds twice looking for Molly and April. I thought they might be at the swimming pool, but the place didn't have one. Before I started knocking on doors, I decided to ask after them at the office.

"I'm still near Winnemucca?"

"Not even close, guy. You're in Utah. Near Provo."

"Provo?"

"Well, yeah. Provo, east of Salt Lake City."

"I was traveling with..."

"Those two darlings. I know."

"Have you seen them?"

"Yeah, mister. They left with their mom. That was their mom, right? She had her own room is why I ask. They loaded up on candy and pop and left with her in the station wagon. Going south I think she said. You owe for the second night."

I paid him for the mysterious second night and started the Lincoln. Across the parking lot, a solo blackbird was perched on a power line. It looked to me like it was eyeing the Lincoln and me. The bird looked capable of flight but undecided. I drove the car in circles in the parking lot to decide if it would run okay. The long, black car felt steady and capable.

The woman who had saved—rescued—Molly and April from me was a mystery. Perhaps a Good Samaritan. That was my hope. I opened the map on the passenger seat and found Provo and saw that I had somehow stayed on course, headed east. Looking up, I saw that, like me, the blackbird had chosen flight.

Scene 12

Finding Ann Arbor was easy, but it took me two days of sleeping in the Lincoln and driving the one- and two-lane country roads before I stumbled onto Our Road.

The last time I'd seen the cottage, it was snow covered. Now in the heat of July, everything was green and overgrown. I guessed at the location of the driveway and turned in. The grass and plants were tall, and the trees hung low. What I could see of the lake was smooth and blue, a few shades darker than the hot summer sky. Climbing out, I was greeted by hot air that made my clothes cling to my skin. I walked onto the property, aiming toward what I believed were the steps down to the cottage. It looked like the place had been abandoned or forgotten by IM's family. I formed a new path down to the small house and walked its side to the back which faced the lake. There were happy, loud voices from the water and motorboats and pontoon boats in the distance going in all directions. I was sweating and slapping at mosquitos, and I turned from the view and tried the back door, finding it locked. I tried the front door on the side of the cottage, and it was locked as well. I walked around to the other side to the kitchen window.

The window latch was set, but the glass had been punched out, and a dirty, gray sweater lay over the sill. I climbed inside using a metal milk crate as a step.

The inside of the cottage was in shambles. It looked like a weekend party fort for teenagers and the full-time residence of mice and rats. The counters were covered with dust, spills, litter, and decoratively placed empty liquor bottles. It was dark save the light from the broken window, so I let more light in by opening the back door facing the lake. I went to the couch and cleared a space by shoving trash and clothing onto the floor. I remembered the couch from years before. It was where I had slept and sat while IM and Heidi Ho carried on up in the loft. I recalled sitting there with my collection of 3D reels and my viewer as snow fell and the cottage grew cold during the winter nights. A second memory played like a newsreel. A long-ago night of reverie and fireworks farther along the lake. A party that had ended in the fiery death of a kind boy who had been trying to bring me food.

The couch had a bad smell—dried urine and dust and alcohol. Listening to the sounds from the lake, I looked around and began a list of what could be done to make the place livable. I saw all I could do and imagined the place and yards cleaned and swept and aired and repaired. I could see the drapes open and the summer light filtering in and scrubbing the room with warmth.

I thought about Molly and April and even Baby Knucklehead. I hoped they were safe with the mystery woman. I bit the inside of my cheek wishing I had fought my curiosity with the little tin bottle. That done, my thoughts turned to Pierce. And Jared. And Baby Ruth.

I left the cottage through the kitchen window after closing and locking the lake-view door knowing I would never return. After climbing to the Lincoln, I opened the trunk and took out all the garden tools I had packed in Hollywood.

It took many short digs and looking around trying to remember before I hazarded my best guess as to where IM was buried.

I began to dig in earnest.

I experienced a new form of gratitude that summer afternoon. The sky was hot and blue, and I could hear passing boats in the cooling breezes. I was grateful that rotted clothing covered my father's bones and stiff muscle tissue. When I located his raised knees, I turned my digging toward the lake in search of his shoes. With his left shoe partially uncovered, I backed up and dug in the area in front of his feet. I was grateful that there was no need to uncover his head, his skull. I was grateful that there was enough room in the hole for me to dig at a new angle. I stopped

GREG JOLLEY

one time, dirty and slick with sweat, and looked at what showed of IM—
his bony thigh and leg bones inside tattered cloth extending out from the
dirt wall. And last, I was grateful when I opened the filthy briefcase before him.

I had worried that the packets of cash would be ruined by years under the soil, but while the money had a foul odor, it was otherwise intact.
I thanked the briefcase for its durability and decided to bring it along.

ACT SEVEN
UNDERWOOD

Flight
*The act or flying; a passing through the air by the help
of wings; mode or style of flying.*

Scene 13

When Mother's mansion sold and all the attached loans were paid off, my offer was accepted on a house in the working town of La Habra. The place had a side-yard swimming pool and was forty minutes from Hollywood. This was the last time during my marriage that I chose where we would live. I learned from the Doc that Mother was distraught about the change, but he promised to keep her calm and medicated.

As moving day drew closer, Hilda and Ira shared their plans to rent themselves a loft apartment in Hollywood, near Regency Films, where he worked as a director of photography.

Moving the boys and Baby Ruth was a breeze, but Mother's transport was difficult. Even though sedated, she was in a wild panic, foul-mouthed, and raging with anger.

"Don't you dare!" she chanted, each time louder.

"It's for the best," the Doc tried. "You'll be fine."

"This can't be! BB! You useless sack of—"

The Doc plunged a second syringe, and she fell back on the gurney.

I was saving her by getting her to a house we could afford. *Maybe* someday she would come around and appreciate what all I had done for her. Maybe crows would learn how to drive automobiles.

With the Doc's medicinal assistance, we moved her in a nonemergency ambulance that had blinds that could be drawn. Prior to her arrival at the La Habra house, the Doc helped me replicate her Hollywood bedroom. We painted her new room—the master bedroom—a deep, pine green and furnished it with some of her furniture from the mansion.

After getting her situated in her room, she pointed from her bed to the balcony over the pool.

"Close those," she muttered, the drugs taking some of the edge off her voice.

Doc drew the heavy curtains once and for good.

Upstairs, beside Mother's room, Baby Ruth had her own room, and Pierce and Jared shared the other. I had the cozy sun porch downstairs behind the kitchen. My first load of wash was the cash, which I laundered on the soft cycle with a half cup of detergent.

Gone were the days of Mother's staff and assistants, although from what I saw, she snared Doc closer. Time and again, I saw him on the stairs to her room delivering meals or carrying his small, black bag. When the ranch-style house beside ours went on the market, he bought it.

In the middle of that year of transition, I was hired by Blue Coast Pictures, which was not in Hollywood but in the practical, low-cost outskirts of Burbank. At Blue Coast—a small studio—I had two jobs. I did rewrites of scene sequences in the writers' office when I wasn't assigned to the second-unit shoots to make rewrites on the fly.

During that first year, I only had to open IM's briefcase one time. Baby Ruth's school counselor asked to meet. Following a review of Baby

Ruth's academic achievements, the counselor laid some brochures on his desk.

"Baby Ruth is both brilliant and curious, but I fear she's wilting in her current life and this school. If you wish to save her from a life of the mundane, I recommend any of these three prep schools."

"Save her," was all I heard.

Two days later, having read about the suggested schools, I paid forward for her first year's boarding and tuition with three packets.

• • • •

JARED SAT beside Baby Ruth in the back seat when I drove her to the train depot, and after curbing her bags, I sat in the automobile while they entered the terminal to say their good-byes. When he returned, he sat up front beside me, dry-eyed and expressionless, and talked conversationally with himself. I noted for the first time on that drive home that he might not be speaking to himself but to the passenger-side mirror.

I spent that same evening in my sun porch sitting before the typewriter on the table at the window. I thought about loading a sheet of paper, but for the longest time—the next year or so—the Underwood grew nothing but dust.

• • • •

PIERCE AND Jared made movies everywhere—in the yards, in the garage, and in the orange grove across the two-lane road. I liked to watch. Pierce directed and operated the viewfinder, and handsome, pensive Jared fulfilled whichever role his brother devised. Ira arranged for an internship for Pierce at his studio, and he began working after school and on weekends. They had him building and moving props that sometimes found their way to our house instead of into the studio's storage. The various film props transformed the pool yard and the boy's homegrown films. At different times, the pool yard resembled a WWII battlefield, a Western cowboy camp with a Styrofoam rock campfire, and the interior of a ship's helm.

With Pierce's school and work schedule, the boys often filmed at night under the stars within the varying types of lighting he borrowed from the studio. I often went to sleep with Pierce's voice directing and Jared either rehearsing his lines or performing them. Other nights, I would sit in my deck chair outside the sun porch and watch their movie making from the shadows. What I admired about Pierce and Jared's moviemaking was their nonuse of film. In fact, they rarely used cameras. Instead, Pierce would form a rectangular viewfinder by touching his thumbs and fingertips. To me, it seemed they were focused on the creativity and the process instead of the end result.

At the beginning of our second year in La Habra, both boys invited me inside their filmset along the far side of the pool. I entered the detailed interior of a yacht, and we sat at the galley table where Pierce lit a lantern. Jared sat so that his eyes were in darkness, and the rest of his lovely face was lit in amber. Pierce told me that he was done with schooling and was taking a full-time job at the studio. He described his choice as risky but making good sense. He wasn't looking for permission, but agreement. I turned my goggles to him and gave him a grin, all my teeth showing.

Scene 14

The seasons changed, and three years unfurled and little changed in our daily lives.

Baby Ruth came home for the first week of November, and like past years, her arrival was a gift. She and Jared and Pierce took up with each other quickly, the boys absorbing her into the crew for their current film, *Sergeant Jared and the Nazis*. She happily applied Jared's battle face makeup and bruises while Pierce talked about the lenses and points of view he wanted to use. I listened from the sun porch, the windows angled open, letting in the colors of their voices and rain and cold air. My three were sitting at the umbrella table back away from the deep end of the pool.

They were planning to film in the fading gray light and continue into the night. Pierce was concerned about running the set lights in the rain.

Baby Ruth reminded the boys—and me, indirectly—that the night's work needed to end early, so we could be up at dawn to celebrate daylight saving time. For the past three years, the changing of the clocks and time had caused my brain to unwind, affecting my motor skills for two days, sometimes three. So my three gathered at least twice a year to linger near me while also making a party of the change.

At dawn, I woke to, "Happy DST!"

My three squeezed into the sun porch carrying breakfast trays, and we sat scrunched, me still in bed, Baby Ruth and Jared sitting on the desk, and Pierce in the desk chair. It was raining, the sound of drops coming in through the angled window. Baby Ruth wore a sheer summer dress and no shoes, jewelry, and any other adornment she had. Jared was still in his battlefield makeup and uniform. My old Tewe director's lens hung from Pierce's neck, sweeping as he talked. He was dressed haphazardly as always—a green and white striped shirt over a pair of red and orange plaid shorts.

Baby Ruth stepped over from the desk and sat beside me and changed the time on my nightstand windup. She handed me the clock, and I held it in both hands as she kissed my brow and suggested I wait an hour before I stood.

I agreed.

"Boob," Pierce commented.

Baby Ruth looked down and covered her budding, errant breast with a tug of her dress top. She gave Pierce her landmark sideways grin and shrug. Jared turned from the mirror, hanging from the back of my bedroom door, his lips whispering. He dropped his worried expression and offered his rare and beautiful smile to Baby Ruth.

We ate breakfast, and they talked, each in their own distinct ways, loudly and happily, mostly about the day's shoot. Pierce was worried about the planned shoot for the day because of the weather, and it was Jared who quietly suggested a change to the storyline. He described a scene of Sergeant Jared still stateside and departing for military service. Pierce fleshed out the idea with specifics, mostly camera angle concerns, and they decided to film in the garage. They invited me to come and watch.

"This will have to be in black and white if we're gonna film in Mother's pink car. We could use BB's, but it's out in the rain."

The black Lincoln was parked in the driveway. I had learned not to garage it during the time change, not wanting my unsteady hands to drive it into the garage door frames. Throughout the past two years, my brain had changed in other ways. Clocks and calendars became suspect. With each daylight-saving-time change came spells of unsettling confusion as though my place on the earth had slid out of kilter.

"I like the idea of black and white," Baby Ruth told Pierce. "Love to see *my* Jared's beautiful face in those hues."

I watched the three of them discuss and work out the last details for the shoot. After we had finished breakfast, Jared and Baby Ruth carried the trays to the kitchen before heading off to join Pierce in the garage.

I got out of bed and had a brief bout of vertigo, my vision flickering like an old movie projector. I stood very still waiting for it to settle. Jared came into the sun porch and stood silently at my side. He took my hand and turned to the pool area. I did the same, and both of us gazed out at the surface of the water, disrupted and electric with raindrops.

I was the first to look away, back to my son's handsome face. He was studying the pool surface, its reflection marred by the rain. His lips were forming silent words. Leaning forward to catch his eye, to nudge his focus, I examined his lovely face with the brown and black smudges of war paint. My darling Jared shook his head, muttered under his breath, and continued to face the pool but turned his eyes and winked at me.

I squeezed his warm hand and panned my head very slowly looking at the change in time on my alarm clock. Five silent minutes later, I gave his hand another squeeze and said, "It's show time."

• • • •

MOTHER'S LINCOLN had years of dust on it and was parked on the right side of the garage on its cracked flat tires. In the space for my automobile, Pierce had set out patio chairs in a row. The big door to my side was open letting the rain in. Jared guided me to a chair, and I sat between Pierce and Baby Ruth. Pierce held his dual-sided clipboard in his lap with the pages on both sides covered with diagrams of overhead camera placements and movements as well as inked notes and arrows.

Baby Ruth had pulled on her royal-blue great coat from school and sat with her bare feet on the seat of her chair, her cocoa knees raised. She was taking bites from a peach and nodding to the one-sided conversation that Pierce was leading. She had a fresh *civilian* shirt for Jared and a damp cloth to remove his battle makeup. Pierce clipped fresh, blank pages to his board and drew as he explored and explained, talking his way through the story and design of what sounded like a new movie, or perhaps a different set of scenes for *Sergeant Jared and the Nazis*. He explained to us the importance of Civilian Jared's departure from his small-town home to the big, new world.

Jared was, as always, listening carefully to his brother while looking over at the pink Lincoln to the door-side mirror. I panned my eyes slowly, and Baby Ruth's free hand lowered from view, taking his. She spoke to me. "BB, Mother cornered me. Yelping from her room to mine."

"And?" Pierce asked.

"The usual. Nonsense. You three. And *your strange moviemaking.*" She mimicked Mother sounding unhinged and hostile. "*God's the important camera.* I believe that was aimed at you, BB. She likes to quote you in her nasty way."

"BB?" Pierce started.

"Dad, please," I said.

"Right. BB, how nuts is she?"

I didn't reply.

"Anyway," Baby Ruth continued. "Before I ditched her, she started in again on the Jared rant."

Baby Ruth laughed before speaking again.

"She's got a new plan for you, my favorite," she said to Jared. "And by the way, you're definitely *not* her favorite."

"Who is?" Pierce chimed while he sketched with a smile in his voice.

Baby Ruth leaned forward to catch Jared's attention which was focused on the automobile door mirror.

"Wants to have you diagnosed."

Pierce laughed loudly. "How's she gonna do that? Hasn't left her room in years."

"You mean her green womb?" Baby Ruth giggled.

Jared smiled in full and turned to her.

"All very interesting, but let's focus, okay?" Pierce instructed.

"Right. Aye, aye, sir," Baby Ruth agreed with her husky laugh.

"We're going to do *Civilian Jared's Departure*, starting with his drive from home to wherever his future is..."

"Not an asylum, okay?" Baby Ruth deadpanned and wiggled her shoulders in delight.

"Okay, yes. Not there. We're going to stay with his planned trip to boot camp. BB?"

"Dad, please."

"Right. I've come up with an idea for camera placement. On your car. Can we?"

Pierce handed me his clipboard, and I studied the top-down view of an accurate drawing of my Lincoln with the driver's door open. There were angled lines from the door to the frame and a camera in silhouette centered on them.

"You can use it," I agreed.

"Swell. I want an exterior shot looking back inside the car. We'll get the car up to high speed and get all the wind washing Civilian Jared. Eighty miles an hour, driving through turns, no. Along the coast."

"The wind will slap, slam that door shut," Baby Ruth observed, leaning over to the drawing. "Or are those metal? Those door braces?"

"Yeah. Not too hard to make those."

"I'd use a car jack," Baby Ruth interrupted. "Bolt it to the frame with the cup thing against the open door."

"That could work," Pierce agreed. "That would let us adjust the angle by cranking the jack."

"Kay, but hey, wait…" Baby Ruth's delicate eyebrows furrowed.

"Okay. Waiting…"

Baby Ruth released Jared's hand and circled Mother's Lincoln with the half-eaten peach. She opened the driver's door, studied it, and looked over the roof to Pierce.

"Pie?" she asked, using her nickname for him. "I didn't get this, but now I do. Didn't see why the jack mattered, but…you're planning to use a real camera?"

I didn't look for Pierce's response because I saw it in Baby Ruth's wise smile.

Jared asked, "And film, too?"

There was silence for another minute save for the patter of rain and a breeze through the big open door. Pierce broke it.

"Not decided on the need for film, but it's a yes on the camera. Sure as hell don't want to hang my ass out in high-speed wind for the shoot."

Baby Ruth circled her chair, got her feet up on it, and retrieved Jared's hand.

"I agree," I offered. "A lot."

"Thanks, BB," Pierce said to his pen and paper. "I'll get this built today, and we'll film tomorrow."

I believe all four of us were staring at Mother's Lincoln. I didn't want to turn and check. Sitting still, perfectly still, felt best. It was Jared who stirred the quiet.

"I'm good with the camera, but no film."

His request was granted without discussion.

• • • •

THE NEXT day, we had warm weather and a white, rain-free sky. My black Lincoln's door was open, the jack had been installed low, so it was easy to step out over. Pierce had finished securing one of his rebuilt 35mm cameras with bolts and nuts and was adjusting the camera, talking, and looking through its viewfinder. I was sitting very still. We had moved our chairs to the driver's side of the automobile. Baby Ruth sat beside me, her bare feet sweeping back and forth just above the dusty concrete floor. Jared was in behind the wheel and listening closely to Pierce directing and instructing him, telling him where to move and not to move and to stay in the frame.

"Jared?" Baby Ruth asked.

He was adjusting the review mirror and replied. "Yes?"

"Do you know how to drive?"

"Sort of."

Baby Ruth laughed.

Pierce cursed then muttered, "BB?"

"Dad, please."

"Right. I'm thinking. We do Jared getting in. Starting the motor and all..."

"And?" Baby Ruth asked.

"The high-speed shot is all about the wind and passing beach and ocean..."

"And?"

"BB? Would you mind? Driving for that shot?"

"If it's later today, yes."

"Still bobble-headed," Baby Ruth explained for me.

"Jared? You okay with using a stunt double?" Pierce asked.

Baby Ruth liked that. She nodded her black hair and gave us her throaty laugh.

"Define high speed?" Jared asked.

"Eighty miles an hour," Pierce answered. "BB at the wheel."

"I'm good with that," Jared approved.

I leaned over slowly and followed his gaze into the rearview mirror.

• • • •

THE *TEST* flight, as Baby Ruth called it, went well. Up to sixty miles per hour. Beyond that, the wind on the camera and open door began to buffet and badly affect the Lincoln's steering. I pulled to the side of Pacific Coast Highway a few miles north of Zuma Beach, and we all climbed out to look at the equipment. The four-bolt camera mount had held, but the camera was tilted.

Pierce took tools and parts from the trunk and went to work, confident he could strengthen the rig. Jared climbed out and crossed the highway and stared out to the sea and surf. Baby Ruth was working with Pierce, making amusing comments. I climbed back in behind the wheel from the passenger side. We had the sun at our backs, and the warm air was saltine scented and whisked by an occasional passing vehicle.

Pierce worked with pieces of metal and bolts and added strength to the rig and adjusted the camera's position forward, so the door blocked more of the wind. Twenty minutes later, he and Baby Ruth placed the tools and parts in the trunk, and we were good to go.

"Another test flight?" Baby Ruth asked.

"Nope," Pierce answered.

"Then?"

"Time to fly. Go get my odd brother."

"With pleasure."

Baby Ruth crossed to the beach and stood beside Jared who was looking at the waves and gesturing as he apparently spoke to the view. She took his hand. They whispered. Then her arm went around his waist, and she turned him back to the highway. She and Jared climbed in the back seat, and Pierce joined them, trailing the cable from the camera to the remote start box.

I started the motor and, like before, drove six miles north, turned around and stopped. The composition, as Pierce explained again, was my hands on the wheel in short, nonfocus, and the windshield, part of the hood, and the ocean in sharp focus. I steered out onto the highway, and we began our fast flight to the south.

At fifty miles per hour, Pierce called into the wind streaming from all four lowered windows.

"On four!"

At sixty-five, he hollered, "Roll it!"

I snuck one quick glance into the mirror. I saw him click the camera start button. My shoe pressed further on the accelerator, and I concentrated on keeping the Lincoln on the road.

At seventy-five, I edged the Lincoln out over to the center line, so I had more room to collect the occasional sway of the one-winged automobile.

At eighty, Jared's voice warbled into the swift wind, "Flying!"

I agreed.

The camera was forgotten.

We were soaring.

I continued to press the pedal, and the Lincoln's steering settled down and became easy to control.

There was a clatter and a crunching explosion in the wind at my hip. The camera had come off and hit the pavement.

"BB! Stop, we lost it!" Pierce cried out.

At ninety-five, we rounded the long, left bend as the highway leaned inland past Point Dume. We rejoined the ocean north of Malibu Beach, streaming south.

Pierce continued to scream and was joined by Baby Ruth.

At one hundred five, the Lincoln was no longer on the pavement. We were lifted off low over the road and beach, passing over houses and the buildings beside the ocean. It felt dangerous to raise my hand, briefly, from the steering wheel, but I did so, bravely, long enough to raise my 3D goggles from my eyes to my brow.

At one hundred twenty, I leaned my shoulders as I decided to turn, and the Lincoln banked in a graceful arc like the other birds above the shore. I made more turns, rising up and downward in the expanding and detailed view.

• • • •

WE TOUCHED down a mile past the Malibu Pier when I lifted off the accelerator. I felt the road connect to the tires with the vibration of the steering wheel in my hands. I began braking the Lincoln to a stop in the beach-side turnout at Las Tunas. We slowed with a long roll to a stop. The Lincoln was pinging, the sunlight was bright, and the pure ocean was a royal blue with stretching lines of white foam.

No one spoke, which was rare, but I heard Baby Ruth barf on the floorboard. I turned around on the seat. She was bent forward, her head on her knees. Pierce was wide-eyed, and his mouth hung open. Jared had his arm across Baby Ruth's back. His hand was clenching Pierce's shirt, and he was staring out along the passenger side, possibly to the highway running south or the mirror on the door. He was talking but making no sound.

"BB?" Pierce said a minute later.

"Dad. Yes?"

"Can we go home now?"

"Home? Okay." I turned the Lincoln around, and we cruised north on Pacific Coast, stopping one time to let Pierce out to collect the main body of the camera and the parts that it had lost on impact.

• • • •

FLIGHT.

Flight didn't find its way into my useless nighttime dreams. In the important dreams, those during the day, flight became a constant. Sometimes with me at the stick, piloting. Other times I was a black seabird.

With my goggles on, I flew when at work at the studio during my lunch breaks. I constantly flew when I was home. I flew the pool area, banking and buzzing the water and my three and their moviemaking.

I could fly best in the sun porch sitting in my chair before the table and my Underwood. At times, I flew at high altitudes and marveled at the minute terrain details far below. Other times, I flew at treetop level skimming my bed and the cityscape of the furniture.

If I chose, I could raise my left hand to my ear and hear a long-lost transistor radio. The station was playing Pierce and Jared and Baby Ruth—their happy and focused, sparkling conversations coming in clear—clear as day.

• • • •

A FEW days later, I was midflight in sunset light along the front of the house, weaving in and out of the pines that led to the front porch, seeing everything in touching detail. That day, I discovered a new ability. I could see sounds like the tire rush of an automobile passing the house on the two-lane road. It was a mixture of silver and gray and transparent like plastic wrap. I could *see* the breeze that was carrying from the orange orchard across the road. When the flavor of citrus entered my nose, my wings shuddered, and I pushed on the stick looking for the first place possible to land and land quickly.

It was a rough touchdown—bouncing with one wing dipping to the side and striking the lawn, spinning me around so that I landed on my side, amidst the pieces and parts of airplane wreckage.

I stayed perfectly still and performed a mental inventory of my body for serious damage. My skin was damp, which was the only effect I could feel. With my head on the grass, I had a sideways view of our front steps and door and Doc's house across the way. I watched the sound of a vehicle pass by on the road and saw the wood on tile scrape our front door opening. Panning my eyes in that direction, I saw Doc step out through our door, spot me, and walk over. I lay still as he lowered down beside me.

"Hey, BB." His voice floated out into the daylight. "Was looking in on your wife."

My goggles were filled with the fine, linear details of Doc's corduroy pants—straight lines that were aimed south to the turn of his knee.

"A couple of things," he went on.

"The medications are no longer effective. I'll need your signatures. I've arranged for her hospitalization. She'll be in a good place with proper care. The best care. She's going to be transported tomorrow. Everything's arranged, and I've set up things so you'll be billed."

It seemed the wind, the breeze, changed directions and also changed color. I could no longer see the scent of citrus. Doc and I were silent for the next two minutes, the quiet disturbed only once by the distant call of Pierce's voice followed by splashing water.

"Here's the other thing," Doc said. "Please sit up."

After panning, testing my head, I rolled onto my rear and sat up on the lawn.

He was offering me an envelope. I took it in my hand and nodded as I read along the lines of the return address and the row of the letters of my name.

"Lovely handwriting, and it's scented," Doc said. "Was hand-delivered by a guy in a suit and a long car."

• • • •

I WENT around to the gate to the side yard and walked along the pool to the sun porch, passing Pierce, Jared, and Baby Ruth who were lying on their beach towels in the cool shade from the angled umbrella. They lay side by side in a row with Baby Ruth in the middle holding both their hands.

I sat at my Underwood table before I took a breath from the envelope. I inhaled with the envelope touching my lips. My body tilted but stayed upright on my chair. I saw the scents of eucalyptus and pine—the flavors of the trees in the Santa Cruz mountains.

I breathed out and opened the envelope and pulled out an invitation printed on heavy, cream stationary.

Dear BB,

I hope this finds you well.

You are cordially invited to a film premiere that I am hosting at my house.

I believe the film will be interesting for you. An inspiring story of rescue if not redemption.

Sincerely,
Ezra Mayer

The date and time followed as well as directions from our house to Ezra's.

Scene 15

The afternoon of the premiere, I told my three that I would be back home later that night. Baby Ruth was looking me over. I had bought new clothes—gray serge pants, a dark gray shirt, and a black vest—and she chirped, "BB's got a date?"

With Mother's recent departure, the three of them had reclaimed the downstairs interior of the house where they sometimes filmed. That afternoon, they were sitting on the tiles of the emptied front room talking about *Jared the AWOL Surf Bum*. I left them to their work and went and climbed carefully into the Lincoln. The directions led me west out of La Habra and eventually to the coast, and, finally, to a twisting, steep driveway.

I parked in the shade of a grove of eucalyptus and thought I might be early or misread the time on the invitation. There was enough parking space for twenty automobiles and mine was the only one. I walked up the hill to the large home with its rows of windows facing the ocean. There was a smooth ramp beside the stairs to the front door. A thin and short owl-faced man watched me climb, and I admired the contrast between his stern expression and his colorful, festive clothing.

"Got your invitation, sir?" he asked in a nasally voice.

I handed him the envelope, and while he looked the white card over, I asked, "Am I too early?"

"No, sir. You're right on time. Let me get the door."

Inside the home, the western wall was a row of windows bordered by pine trees. The beautiful, blue Pacific lay below the endless, blue sky. The large room had many low cream couches and white tables. The doorman followed me into the room. He extended his hand to an elegant buffet on white linen tables.

"Please, help yourself," he said and disappeared.

I was thirsty but not hungry. I walked to the open bar and looked at the rows of liquor bottles—and the side tray of little tin bottles and a stack of white satin handkerchiefs—and selected a cola from the ice. I stood sipping with the scents of pine and eucalyptus sparkling in my brain.

"BB, I'm so pleased." I heard and turned around.

Ezra Mayer had not aged well. He looked sickly yet happy in his Hawaiian shirt, tan shorts, and sandals. He had thinned significantly, and his skin was an unhealthy, pasty white.

"Welcome to our beach place," he said, crossing the white tiles to me, his trembling hand out.

I asked Ezra the same question I had asked the doorman.

"No, you are on time."

"Will there be other guests attending?"

"No, you're our only guest tonight. Come, something to dine on?" He gestured to the silver platters of meats, fruits, and vegetables.

I raised my cola can. "No, thank you."

"It's been quite a long time." He smiled, and I noted the spittle on the left side of his lips. There was a white handkerchief in the front pocket of his floral shirt, and I wondered if it was damp.

"Come," he said, and I followed his slow walk in the other direction. He led the way up a wide hall that resembled a theatre hallway with thin tables and love seats. I saw the ghosts on the walls, the dust shadows of once-hanging pictures or paintings. Candles in glass lighted the hall. Ezra walked ahead of me, talking softly. It wasn't clear if he was talking to himself or me. I heard him mumble Mumm's stage name "Elizabeth Stark" one time as we walked deeper. He waved to a room with two sixteen-foot mahogany doors. We entered, and he parted the heavy gold curtains that hung between the doorway and the theatre.

The room angled downward and was lit from lamps high up between gold buntings on both walls. The decline to the stage held thirty comfortable chairs each with a side table. Ezra led the way down the center aisle. He pointed his thin, trembling finger to the bottom row.

"Our screening is for you." His voice was shaky.

I squinted into the darkness. There appeared to be a rise of equipment, spare projectors and such, against the wall. I stepped past him, and he added, "End of the row, please."

Ezra followed me to the base of the stage and along the chairs and tables to what I then saw was tall and varied medical devices, some on tripods. "There," he instructed when I stood before the chair next to the equipment. The theatre lights dimmed to complete darkness. I sat down and watched him leave, thinking he would take the seat beside mine.

The devices were making two distinct, soft sounds—one was sucking, breathlike, and the other was giving off a whirring of small gears and a blinking, blue light. I gave up on trying to decide what the machines were doing. I assumed they provided care for Ezra.

In the darkness, I saw that the seat beside mine was occupied. That blue lightbulb blinked again, and I made out a petite woman dressed all in black including a black hat with a matching veil. She was sitting low and still. The lights in the theatre warmed for a few seconds before dimming away signaling show time. I turned and watched the tall, gold curtains draw across the stage slowly. There was the movie screen.

Nothing happened for the next three minutes. No projector flickers, no sound, no soundtrack, only the clicks and breaths of the medical machines. Then a voice, faint, but also crisp, with a British lilt said to me from my right, "It's 3D, love. Did you bring your goggles?"

There was a scent to her words. A blend. Pine and eucalyptus.

"I'm wearing them, yes."

The screen went white with projector light, and in that light, I watched the woman raise her black-speckled veil. With trembling fingers, she raised a pair of goggles from her side table. I watched her hands hesitate and shake. I looked at her face.

I know I took a deep breath—seeing and recognizing Mumm's face, and seeing the horrible, melted damage that had been done to it. Her nose, cheek, and ear were destroyed from what must have been chemicals or fire or both.

I breathed deeply again, my chest and my belly clenching.

All I could say was her name.

She raised the goggles to her face, her wavering fingertips attempting to put them on. I watched her struggle and reached over, saying, "Let me help."

"Yes, please."

As tenderly as I knew how, I placed the goggles on above the scarred tissue of her nose before gently looping the ear grips into her hair.

"It has been awhile, love," she said softly, her head tilting to me.

Her hand reached for mine over the side table, her skin a creamy pale. I took it lightly in mine.

"I hope you enjoy," she said in a playful voice, followed by a cough. "Last film I was in," she added after clearing her throat.

I found my voice. "Which one is it?"

She gave my hand a soft grip by way of explanation, and thirty seconds later, the color on the movie screen changed to black. A cloud of white angel dust fell. The dust condensed, and over the next twenty seconds, it formed white letters on the black background: *Savior*.

In 3D, the title extended out into the theatre, against my chest, embracing my head. The title dissolved to minute snowflakes that drifted to the stage floor and into my hands, forming small mounds. I sat inside the white dust of words as a new cloud of white dispersed and formed the credits.

"Elizabeth Stark" appeared beside her character's name, "Mumm."

The meadow appeared with the ocean beyond. The image dissolved, and there was Mumm, two stories tall, filling the oxygen particles of the theatre. She was sitting in the sweeping, gold grass. I extended my free hand and brushed the straw away from my face.

I listened to the soundtrack, the winds from the trees and the sea. I watched the different currents of song change hue and blend. Mumm's eyes were dreamy and sad and thoughtful. The back of my white shirt appeared as I entered the meadow. I watched myself walk to her, my left hand low and clenched. There we were, Mumm and I, side by side from many years ago. The length of rope was there in my hand, but not yet visible in the shot.

In the theatre, with our hands joined, we kept our goggles to the movie. Mumm and me, immersed in the short story of saving.

• • • •

WHEN THE film ended, the lights remained off. Two women with pinpoint lights appeared from behind the medical equipment. One of them disconnected the devices, and Mumm was wheeled away, her chair on silent casters. She appeared to be sleeping. Her veil was still raised, but her chin was down to her chest. I watched her as she was rolled through curtains on the side wall. When the curtains closed, I waited a minute, listening to nothing, and left the theatre.

The silhouettes on the hallway walls had been covered. Film posters and large still photographs had been put back up. Each was elegantly framed and had a cloth matte and featured Elizabeth Stark and her films. In the front room, I was greeted by light from the big windows. I watched the last of the orange sun sink into the royal-blue sea.

Ezra stood beside the front door talking to the festively dressed doorman. As I approached, his trembling fingers slid his white cloth into his shirt pocket. The doorman got the door, and Ezra and I stood on the front porch in the failing light, both of us looking down across the well-maintained landscaping. I hadn't said a word since the film ended and had no words at that moment either.

"Thank you," Ezra said to the view.

I didn't reply, so he went on.

"She only has a little time. I've tried to save her—well, no, I *have* saved her. I know you once tried…"

A flock of snipes lit and flew across the sky, headed south, possibly for the row of eucalyptus trees or the ocean miles away.

"Drive carefully, please," Ezra said and sniffled.

The chatting birds swarmed past the trees. I retrieved the Lincoln's keys from my vest pocket.

I had nothing to ask or say, so I walked down and across to the Lincoln, watching the snipes fly to the ocean, becoming smaller and smaller until they disappeared.

Scene 16

I'm sitting here at the keys of my Underwood wondering about flight in 3D. Maybe someday we will find a way to place cameras on little wooden airplanes and fly the rooms and cities, forests and coastlines. Somehow, maybe like television, people will view and control the flight, the viewfinder, from below. For now, I'm good with pulling on my goggles and flying the black Lincoln with all the different colors of wind coming in through the jacked-open door.

Doc came by a half hour ago, entering the sun porch looking uncertain and undone. His voice was unhinged. I didn't know the reason for the visit, so I sat there on my chair and viewed and listened. I nodded along the lines of his voice which was running like errant film spilling from a broken projector. He talked about Mother's return and his plans and worries.

"Her treatments aren't completed."

I didn't have anything to say about that and swept my goggles back and forth along his chatter until he handed me a letter. I recognized the handwriting and my name and address.

When Doc was spent, fully unwound, I guess, he left. I could see his trailing words like the flickering of movie credits at the end of a film. His voice had appeared in black and white whereas the voices of my three were in color, each one a different shade.

The sun porch was warmed with golden light, and the sky out above the pool was a cloudless blue. I saw Jared's voice appear, royal blue in fine print, dancing with the cream and cinnamon and peach of Baby Ruth's short laughter. Pierce chimed in, a march of greens and orange words. My head was sweeping fast along the lines of their three beautiful voices along the different and crossing streams.

When the music of their conversations dissolved from the angled window, I opened the envelope. Inside was a three by five card with a single sheet of paper folded behind it. The card was an invitation to the memorial for Elizabeth Stark and below was the location and date and time and a reminder to bring the invitation to be sure to be allowed in. There was going to be a retrospective along with the service. Formal attire was recommended.

I swept my nodding goggles along the lines of Ezra's handwriting on the second page and learned that Mumm had been buried in her home village in the UK. He had traveled with her to her final resting place.

I breathed from the pages before folding them back inside the envelope. It was a subtle flavor of dust and papyrus. I laid the envelope on my table beside the Underwood in front of the open box of white typing paper. I would not be attending.

It came to me then that I had been wrong when I told the boys and Baby Ruth that God was the big director.

"He's not. We are," I typed on the Underwood. That seemed to explain His affection for us. He leaves the acting and directing to us, enjoying our many choices and wishes. And why? He loves our stories.

The blue lines of Jared's voice danced across my goggles from poolside—a three-word exclamation of humor and bemusement that sounded scripted.

I watched my darling Pierce's caustic instructions enter the flow, a mix of lime and tangerine. The colors weaved and swam and dissolved into new shades of delighted laughter.

· · · ·

INSIDE THE front pocket of my black suit pants are the keys to the Lincoln. There is no need to worry anymore. No rescue required.

Earlier this morning, Pierce brought me breakfast laid out on a cutting board. Toast and eggs and a cup of something. Jared followed his brother and stood in the doorway watching the dresser mirror and me. At Pierce's verbal nudge, Jared entered and offered me the orange in his young, tan hand.

"We picked it for you from the orchard across the road," Pierce explained.

I looked at the orange in my steady hands.

I didn't peel it. I twisted and broke it open in half and raised the fragrant meat to my face. My fingers became slick with juice as I breathed in deep.

My chair fell on its side, and I gathered myself up slowly. My head must have hit the floor hard because my goggles were askew. I corrected their angle and set the chair upright.

I'm typing again, my view panning left to right and then back, flying slowly and low over these words.

I might be done here. Not saved, but free.

Pierce and Jared and Baby Ruth are in the pool. I can see the sparkling water in sunlight and their laughter and wit and kindness. My three. I believe that I've saved each one of them. Saved them by giving them the freedom of forward flight.

I use my bare foot to nudge IM's briefcase full of cash. There's enough there for Pierce and Jared and Baby Ruth to fly for years.

I'm almost done with this Underwood. I've got the keys to the black seabird and its jacked-open door.

I'm eager for flight.

My own.

My last.

Fast along and over the blue Pacific.

The End

ACKNOWLEDGMENTS

Stephanie Jorgensen, the best editor on the planet

Robert A. Jolley, the other best editor on the planet

Shoot First! Assignments of a Newsreel Camera-man
by Ronnie Noble

A Seabee's Story
by Lieutenant Colonel George A. Larson, USAF (Ret.)

The Seabees of World War Two
by Commander Edmund Castillo, USN

Looking Back
by Thomas P. Hennings

Northfield Harvest
edited by Wystan Stevens

Edwin Eugene Mayer

William B. Gruber

"Beautiful World" (Alternate Mix) by Colin Hay

Charles Addams

The mind of Sarah Silverman

The style of Harrison Steampunk Weissenberger

ABOUT THE AUTHOR

Greg Jolley earned a Master of Arts in Writing from the University of San Francisco and lives in the very small town of Ormond Beach, Florida. When not writing, he is a student and researcher of historical crime, primarily those of the 1800s.

CPSIA information can be obtained
at www.ICGtesting.com
Printed in the USA
BVHW030721071119
563135BV00003B/18/P

9 781643 970042